Vengeance Is Mine

Vengeance Is Mine

MARGARET E. KELCHNER

Beacon Hill Press of Kansas City
Kansas City, Missouri

Copyright 1995
by Beacon Hill Press of Kansas City

ISBN 083-411-6103

Printed in the
United States of America

Cover Design: Paul Franitza
Cover Illustration: Keith Alexander

Library of Congress Cataloging-in-Publication Data
Kelchner, Margaret E.
  Vengeance is mine / Margaret E. Kelchner.
      p.   cm.
   ISBN 0-8341-1610-3
    1. United States—History—Civil War, 1861-1865—Veterans—Fiction.
2. Man-woman relationships—South Carolina—Charleston—Fiction.
3. Charleston (S.C.)—History—Fiction. 4. Revenge—Fiction. I. Title.
PS3561.E3833V46   1995   95-26450
813'.54—dc20   CIP

10   9   8   7   6   5   4   3   2   1

About the Author

Although all her novels thus far are set in the past, Margaret E. Kelchner believes firmly that humanity's basic needs, emotions, and behavior have remained constant throughout history. It is these facets of the human condition that she uses in demonstrating God's unchanging grace, His forgiveness, and His loving involvement with individuals.

"People still have bitterness, jealousy, intense love, hatred, distrust," she comments. "I try to turn my readers' minds toward God to help them see how people of the past got through their problems by looking to God for help, becoming stronger persons because of those hard times."

As with her previous three novels published by Beacon Hill Press of Kansas City, which include *Father of the Fatherless* (1993), *A Shadow from the Heat* (1994), and *Nightsong* (1995), Mrs. Kelchner has visited and researched the region that serves as the setting for *Vengeance Is Mine*. "My husband and I spent several weeks in the Savannah-Charleston area," she explains. "I came up with the idea for this novel while walking the streets of Savannah and going in and out of the old homes there. I have a vivid imagination and like to try stepping back in time. In Charleston we visited the marketplace, the docks, the lowlands, crossed the Edisto River, and saw many sights that I included in this story."

Three characters in this latest novel are based on historical figures Mrs. Kelchner learned about when she and her husband visited Fort Pulaski National Monument, near Savannah, Georgia. The characters of Clemson, Jack Brevard, and Tom Searles are spin-offs of historical figures involved in a similar episode during the Civil War, in which three Southern soldiers escaped from Fort Pulaski, only to be betrayed by one of the three.

Explaining what she wishes the reader to experience from her novels, Mrs. Kelchner comments, "I want the reader to realize that people in the past had some bad things happen to them, but a seed of faith helped many of them find their way out as they looked to God for answers."

Mrs. Kelchner and her husband, Raymond, have 3 children, 9 grandchildren, and 12 great-grandchildren. The couple spend the summers in Anderson, Indiana, and the winters near Phoenix, at the foot of the Superstition Mountains.

1

$\mathcal{H}$EAVY FOG HUNG LOW TO THE GROUND, dripping from the moss hanging in ghostly live oak trees. A rider and his horse made their way through the empty, silent streets of Savannah in the dim light of dawn. Just past the old pirate's house, where marauders sneaked in for a night of revelry, Captain Andrew Jackson Brevard pulled up to take one last look across the Savannah River at the dark shadow of what had been Fort Pulaski but now lay in ruins. Twenty years had been spent building its massive structure, surrounded by a wide moat. Boasted by the South to be impregnable, the Federalist artillerymen had wreaked havoc, reducing it to rubble during the War Between the States. Turned into a prison for Confederates captured by the Union forces, it had become a pit for miserable, malnourished, mistreated humanity.

Jack's younger brother had died there at the hands of a brutal, unscrupulous guard who had beaten the boy unconscious until he fell from the rampart into the moat filled with gators. The man had been responsible for two deaths in the family, Jack thought bitterly, for his mother died grieving for her son.

Well, at least that score had been settled. The guard had sealed his death warrant as surely had he pierced himself with a sword. The Union officers had simply turned their backs that dark and deadly night.

Pushing the unpleasant memories from his mind, Jack urged his mount on toward the west, where he turned into the road leading north toward Charleston. He did not look back. Of all Colonel Stothard's men, he was the only one who had not married and settled down. The old days were over, and no longer would they ride the trails together. He would miss the nights spent around a campfire, he admitted silently. Like a restless, driven man, he knew it was time to ride on.

The letter in his pocket had given him the incentive to do so, and it was now very much on his mind. Since the war, he had not known if the writer, Thomas Searles, was even alive.

His thoughts went back to that fateful night he and big Tom Searles had made their escape from Fort Pulaski. As they had plotted their escape, one of the other prisoners, a man named Clemson, had overheard their whispered talk. He insisted he be allowed to go or threatened to expose their plan. Caught in the act, reluctantly they had agreed to take him along, though neither trusted him.

Crawling through the carefully made earthen tunnel, the three desperate men had fearfully swum the alligator-infested moat to make their way to the waist-deep, murky waters of the tidal basin surrounding the fort. The going had been difficult, Jack remembered with a grimace. Their feet had been sucked into the mud, making progress slow.

With daylight pressing hard upon them, all that had stood between them and freedom was a chance Union patrol boat. They froze, waiting for the boat to pass, hoping their presence would go undetected by the guard standing with his back to them. All would have gone well had Clemson remained silent. Instead, he had shouted, "Don't shoot! We'll surrender!"

Searles and Jack had made a mad dash to elude being caught but were soon overtaken. While Clemson had gone free, pledging allegiance to the North, Searles had been sent to the dreaded Perryville Prison farther north, and Jack had been returned to Fort Pulaski to suffer in solitary confinement. Later he had successfully escaped, rejoining Colonel Stothard and his men, vowing someday to keep the pact he had made with Searles to track down Clemson and make him pay for his betrayal.

Until he had received Tom's letter a few days ago, Clemson's whereabouts had been unknown. Overjoyed at hearing his old friend was alive, Jack nevertheless shuddered as the ghosts of the past raised their ugly heads at the mention of Clemson's name.

Clemson had been a Southern sympathizer, joining the Confederate cause, but when the tide of the war turned against the South, he lost his zeal for the romance of fighting a lost cause. To save his skin he became a turncoat, declaring allegiance to the North and joining the Union forces.

Clemson had used Jack and Tom to further his own plan. They had been helpless to do anything about it, Jack remembered with bitterness, but now the day for vengeance had come. It was Clemson's turn to suffer.

The sun came up in a murky sky, and its early heat soon burned the fog away. Up to this point, Jack had been content to bury himself in thought, allowing his horse, Prince, to set his own pace, but now he urged the large chestnut into a faster gait. By midday he ignored the gnawing pains in his stomach, realizing he would have to keep moving to make it halfway before darkness overtook him.

In the late afternoon Jack cast a speculative glance at the clouds building to the west and hiding the sinking sun. Looking around for some sort of shelter, he found nothing but open pine country. There was nothing to do but keep riding in hopes he would come across a homestead up ahead.

He pulled his slicker from the saddlebag and put it on. A strong gust of wind signaled the approaching storm, swaying the pines with its force. A streak of lightning lit up the dark, boiling clouds, followed by a reverberating crash of thunder. Prince tossed his head and rolled his eyes.

"It's all right, old fellow—we'll find a place to stop here soon," Jack said, laying a steadying hand on the thoroughbred's neck.

A tiny pinpoint of light appeared in the distance. Peering through the gathering darkness, he tried to discern whether it was a campfire or a house. He coaxed Prince into a full gallop in that direction, keeping his eyes on the faint beam that would appear and disappear behind the foliage. Riding into a group of oak trees, Jack feared he had ridden too far when a loud crackle of lightning split the sky overhead, illuminating the terrain. Just ahead, Jack saw a lowland shack with a porch across the front, and he sent Prince lunging forward. Suddenly the light he had seen vanished.

"Halloo, the house!" Jack called out, pulling up, but no answer was forthcoming.

Puzzled, he slipped from the saddle to lead Prince around to the back in search of shelter. A rundown barn would barely provide cover for Prince, but it was better than nothing.

"Sorry, old fella—I better leave that saddle on," Jack murmured to the horse, giving him a pat on the rump. "I may have to leave here in a hurry."

Loosening his gun in its holster, he headed toward the house. The electrical display of the storm kept the sky lit up continuously now, and he saw a dark face quickly withdraw from the window.

Suddenly realizing he could be in danger, Jack drew his weapon and made swift strides to press close against the building. Heavy drops of water hit the tin roof like bullets and spattered in the dry, sandy soil around him. Knowing the noise would conceal the sound of his movement, he made his way around the corner and up onto the porch.

The door was ajar, and he felt the hair stand up on the back of his neck. Whoever was inside the dark room would have the advantage unless he could cause a diversion. Glancing around for something to throw, he reached for a stick of wood lying nearby and tossed it into the room. There was a grunt of pain. Crouching low, Jack burst through the door, crying in a thunderous tone, "Put your hands up!"

"I ain't doin' nothin' wrong, no suh," came a quavering, frightened voice from the dark.

"How many are you?"

"Jus' me, suh—jus' me!"

"Where's the light?"

"It's on de table."

"Light it," Jack ordered above the roar of the rain on the corrugated metal roof.

"Can't do dat. I only found one match, and I already used dat."

Jack reached into his pocket with his left hand to pull out a match. Striking it on the wall, he held it up to see a frightened black man, who he would guess to be in his early 20s, cowering in the opposite corner. His lip was bleeding, giving evidence where the piece of wood had hit. A battered lantern was sitting on a dilapidated table in the center of the small room.

"Get over here and raise the glass," he directed cautiously, waving his gun.

The young man complied with shaking hands. In the circle of light, each sized up the other.

"What's your name?" Jack asked more gently.

"Je—Jess."

"What are you doing here, Jess?" Jack asked, glancing around the room. There was no evidence the man had been here long.

"I been runnin'," the man replied, his eyes never leaving the gun.

"What are you running from?"

"Dey wuz gonna tar 'n' feather me—'n' I didn't steal no horse—no suh, I didn't. So I took off an' I been runnin' long time!" His round face worked as he slowly backed away from the threatening barrel of the gun.

"How long has it been since you've had something to eat?" Jack asked, slipping the gun in its holster.

"Long time, suh."

"Well, Jess, you have nothing to fear from me. I'm just riding through and needed shelter from the storm. Soon as this rain lets up some, I'll get my supplies from the saddlebags and we'll fix some food. It's been a long while since I've eaten too."

"Iffen you'll shed dat slicker, I'll fetch de bags now," Jess offered hopefully, anticipating something to eat.

Jack Brevard studied the anxious face before him, and a fleeting emotion stirred deep within him. He did not pause to analyze the feeling but slipped out of the wet slicker and handed it to Jess. Not being one to trust people he did not know, he was surprised at his own action.

Jess donned the rain gear and was gone only a few moments, returning with his face shining and eyes aglow.

"Whoa!" he whistled at Jack. "Dat's some piece of hoss flesh out dere. Yas suhree! Ya sho' got ya some fine animal!" He lay the saddlebags on the floor beside Jack, who was down on his knees laying a fire in the makeshift fireplace. "Ain't seen de likes o' him since my pappy worked fer a man down Savannah way by de name of Cuhnel Stothard. Yas suh, dat man sho' loved hosses more'n any man I ever seen."

Jack's head snapped up at the mention of Colonel Stothard's name, and he gave Jess a searching glance.

"Your father worked for the colonel?"

"Yas suh. 'Til he got a notion he wanted a homestead of his own down here in de lowlands. He raised some indigo and rice. Did right fine too, 'til Mr. Clem came 'n' told my pappy he wuz a squattin' on his land. My pappy told him he had papers, but Mr. Clem say dey wuz worthless. He told Pappy he'd overlook it iffen he wanted t' stay 'n' work de land fer 'im."

"What did your father do?" Jack asked, measuring coffee into a pot of water.

"Well, weren't much else fer a black man t' do with my mama and all us mouths to fill," Jess answered, his voice taking on a bitter note. He paused a moment, listening to the drops of water falling from the limbs overhead and hitting the tin roof.

"Lookin' back, I reckon Pappy knowed his life weren't worth much aft' dat," Jess mused out loud. "Twarn't long 'til dey come fer my pappy, ridin' in at night. Dat's de last I ever seen 'im. Mama 'n' us children wuz turned out."

"Who owns this land?" Jack asked with casual interest, laying some biscuits in a greased skillet over the coals. He placed a lid on top and sat back on his heels to study his companion's face.

"Mr. Clem," Jess answered, gesturing around the room. "Dis wuz my pappy's place. I come here 'cause I knowed dey won't 'spect it."

Jack frowned at this remark but held his tongue. This would be the very place Jess's enemies would look for him. Only the ferocity of the storm had delayed their arrival, he guessed, but come they surely would. He lowered his eyes to hide the truth, and a coldness stole over him. Only he stood between Jess and the terrible fate that awaited him. But what could he do against so many? he thought. He scratched the new beard on his face. He'd be glad when the time came to shave it off. It itched, and food got stuck in the whiskers.

He got to his feet and went to the door to look out. The storm was over, and only a light rain continued to fall. Stepping out to the porch, Jack took a long draught of cool, sweet, rainwashed air into his lungs. All he could hear in the night was the gentle drip of the rain. He would have to sleep light, if at all, for the wet ground would muffle their approach.

Turning back into the room, he found Jess sitting immobile, staring into the fire, no doubt reliving happier times spent there. Jack pulled the pan of bread from the coals. Taking two tin plates and cups from his pack, he filled the cups with hot coffee, divided the biscuits on each plate, and handed one to the grateful Jess.

While they ate in silence as hungry men do, Jack's mind was busy on the problem at hand. To avoid violence he could hide Jess and try to convince them he was alone and only seeking shelter from the storm.

"Jess, is there a place you can hide around here?"

"Use t' crawl 'neath de back porch when I wuz a chil'. I's a lot bigger 'n dat now," Jess answered, laying his plate aside.

"You better check it out, for sure as anything they'll be coming for you tonight. Make sure there's no varmints there, 'cause you're going to be in a hurry and won't have time to say 'Scat!'" Jack instructed with dry humor.

He picked up the utensils and went out to the porch to rinse them off under a drip from the roof. When he returned, Jess was gone, and he could hear him moving around in the dark. He stepped to the back door.

"Jess, make sure you don't make any tracks in the wet sand," he cautioned.

"I knows, suh—I knows," came a hoarse whisper from the shadows.

Jack packed the plates and cups back in his pack; then he looked around for any other telltale evidence. Only his set of wet boot prints was visible on the wood. Satisfied that everything was in order, he doused the fire, then blew out the lantern. Through the open door he could see the clouds were moving out, leaving a clear, starlit sky. The dim light of the night sky would give him the advantage over those riding in.

Taking his revolver from its holster, Jack sat down against the wall opposite the door where he could see out into the night. A bare foot scraped on the floor, and Jess grunted as he felt his way in the dark.

"I'm right here, Jess. Did you get yourself set up?"

"Yas suh. I can't squeeze 'neath dat porch no more. I had t' loose some of dem boards so I can drop in. It's dry under dere. Only thin'—I's jest hopin' dere's none of dem fleas left t' eat on me. Dat ol' dog of Pappy's usta sleep under dere."

Jess's comment was met with amused silence as the two of them sat quietly, looking out into the night. Jack suddenly sucked in a deep breath as a thought pressed its way into his consciousness: Jess better get into hiding now! When they come, the riders would encircle the house to prevent his escape.

"Jess, you better get into your place now," Jack whispered, giving an urgent nudge. "When they come, there'll be no time.

They'll see you. Hurry! And don't come out, no matter what happens to me!"

Jess scrambled to obey, and although some time went by, it seemed only moments before Jack saw a faint glimmer of light off through the trees. It disappeared, and he saw it no more. They were coming.

Jack got to his feet, listening for the slightest sound, eyes studying the shadow of every bush and tree. Did he hear the blow of a horse? Stepping to the door, he made out the dim outline of a man on a horse and then another, no more than 30 yards away. It surprised him that they had gotten so close without his hearing their approach. He ran to the rear.

"Jess! Don't make a sound. They're out there," Jack warned in a loud whisper. "Remember—stay put!" Backing into the house, he put on his hat to cover his face. Just as well if no one saw him, he thought. He took his stand just inside the front door out of the line of fire.

There was the squeak of leather and muffled hoofs as they moved in closer, surrounding the house. Quickly, torches were lit, and Jack could see his adversaries in bold relief.

"All right, ya may as well come on out—we've got ya surrounded!" a harsh voice called out.

"Hold your fire, gents—I'm just a pilgrim takin' shelter here from the storm!" Jack shouted back in a low grating tone to disguise his voice.

"Step out then, 'n' let's take a look at ya!"

Jack loosely holstered his gun and stepped out onto the porch. There was silence as the spokesman looked him over. He was a big, burly man with a long-handled moustache. Unable to see the man's eyes beneath the brim of his hat, Jack focused his gaze on another man silhouetted against the sky behind him. The figure seemed familiar, but he could not see the man's face in the shadows.

"Where ya headed, stranger?" the leader barked.

"Who wants t' know?"

"Nevah yuh mind! I'll ask the questions here. Where ya headed?"

"Charleston," Jack drawled tersely in the same low tone. "I got business there."

"Who ya got in there with ya?"

"Nobody but me and what varmints have taken t' livin' here; ya'll are welcome t' light and take a look," Jack drawled amiably, his hand resting near his weapon.

The leader shifted his position in the saddle and spat into the dirt, giving the man behind him a dark glance. At the nod of the other fellow, he gave the order.

"You 'n' you, take a look around," he ordered two men.

While they waited for the men to search the premises, Jack stood in a seemingly relaxed position with his back against the wall. He studied the faces of the men in the circle of light. One of them let out a curse when the torch he held burned his fingers, bringing a loud guffaw from a couple of the others as he fanned the injured member. A motion from the man in the shadows quickly silenced them, drawing Jack's attention back to him. Something about the way he sat his horse seemed vaguely familiar. Who was he? His thoughts were interrupted by the men stomping out the door beside him.

"Like he says, there ain't nobody 'round here but him 'n' a horse ya never seen the likes of," one spoke up, climbing into the saddle. "Maybe ya oughta take the horse as a payment for room 'n' board! Haw! Haw!"

Jack stiffened at his remark, but whatever he was about to say was cut short by the spokesman for the group.

"We're on the trail of a thief, mistah—no offense meant," he growled, throwing his torch to the ground. "If ya'll see 'im, bring 'im in."

"Who should I ask fer?" Jack responded, his eyes on the man behind him.

"Any man at Clemdenin Hall. They'll know what t' do."

Jack watched until they had ridden away into the night, then went out to kick wet sand over the burning torches. Returning to the house, he was about to enter when he sensed, more than saw, that something was not right. Slipping silently around the house, he found Jess leading Prince out of the shelter and drew his gun.

"I wouldn't do that, Jess—don't make me have to shoot you," he said quietly. "Now drop the reins and step away."

When the young man had complied, Jack whistled to Prince, who came trotting to his side. "You wouldn't have gotten far anyway," Jack said curtly. "Prince doesn't take kindly to strangers. Why were you trying to run away from me?"

"I heard ya ask who ya should brin' me to," Jess sneered. "I shudda knowed I can't trus' no white man."

"And you thought I would turn you over to them, huh? Even after I fed you and saved your hide?" Jack waved the gun toward the door. "Get on in the house so I can talk to you without someone taking a potshot at us."

Waiting until Jess started in ahead of him, Jack followed, keeping the gun handy. "We won't light the lamp," he said. "Some of them might circle back, and we'd be sitting ducks. It's best you leave tonight anyhow. Head for Charleston." He pulled the letter from his pocket and tore off the address. "Take this and look up Thomas Searles. Tell him Captain Jack Brevard sent you, and he should take care of you until I come. Go straight there and wait for me. If these men catch you, they'll kill you."

"Yas suh, Marsa Jack!" Jess exclaimed gratefully, cramming the piece of paper into his pants pocket.

"I'm not your master. You're a free man. Take care and keep to the shadows so you'll not be seen. Oh yes—here's a little money for food if you need it." Jack pulled some coins from his pocket.

"Thank ya, suh—uh, Cap'n."

"Now, let me look around before you leave here."

Jess hovered near the door, fear almost paralyzing him. The thought of being run down by the vigilantes struck terror to his heart, but he had no place to hide. Run he must. The captain's sudden appearance brought assurance to him.

"Keep a sharp eye," Jack said. "Don't go by the road. Take to the fields where there's cover. And, Jess," Jack said as he gave Jess's shoulder a squeeze, "I knew your father. He was a good man, and I want you to have a chance to be like him. Now go! If they catch up with you within earshot, yell as loud as you can. I'll come running! Wait! Take off that red shirt, or you'll be seen for sure."

Jess hurriedly stripped off his shirt, dropping it to the floor, then disappeared into the night. Jack sat on the step for a long time, hearing only the song of the tree frogs and the sound of rain dripping from the trees. Picking up the telltale shirt, he looked around for a place to hide it, finally choosing to drop it through the boards Jess had loosened.

Taking his saddlebags, he decided to take his chances with Prince for the night. He stretched out on a dry spot, but sleep evaded him. He found himself listening for the cry of a man hunted like an animal.

SEVERAL HOURS HAD PASSED when Jack felt an uneasiness come over him. A sixth sense told him he had better move out fast. Practiced fingers checked the cinches with unseeing accuracy. With ears up and eyes looking off into the night, Prince seemed to sense his master's urgency, stamping his feet impatiently in the soft sand. Jack moved cautiously, and when all was in readiness, he led Prince quietly through the deeper shadows into a thicket of trees he had noticed earlier. He paused again to listen for the slightest sound. What it was he expected to hear he was not sure. Was it just his nerves?

Placing a hand over Prince's soft nose, Jack guided the animal in a wide circle toward the road leading north to Charleston. Looking back, he saw a pinpoint of light appear through the trees. As he stepped into the saddle, he watched in horror as fire and smoke lit up the night sky. Someone had meant for him to be in that fire.

"Come on, boy—let's make tracks," he urged, flipping the reins.

The big thoroughbred stretched into a full gallop as man and horse moved as one through the darkness. Jack gave Prince his head until he was sure enough distance was between him and his enemies. Then he slowed him to a comfortable lope.

There was no doubt in his mind that someone wanted him dead. But who? The man who had seen Prince? Could be. He had known of men who killed for the sake of a good horse. But the image of the rider in the shadows stayed in his mind, and intuitively he felt that man was the real enemy.

Dawn came agonizingly slow, and Jack was glad when there was sufficient light to see the road ahead and behind. However, with the break of the late-summer day, a stiff breeze moved a low-hanging fog inland, making it impossible to see very far in either direction. His thoughts turned to Jess, and he wondered if he had made it to safety. At least this fog would provide cover for the young man fleeing for his life.

Several hours passed before Jack allowed himself the luxury of getting out of the saddle to stretch his legs. Prince took advantage of the moment, cropping at the sweet, tender grass along the sandy road. Though it was approaching midmorning, the sun had not yet burned through the fog. Moisture dripped from the pines and shrubs nearby. Even his clothing felt damp, and the cool wind blowing in off St. Helena Sound added to his discomfort.

Something hot sounded good to him at that moment, but he suppressed the urge to build a fire. He would feel better when he was among friends. If his reckoning was accurate, Parker's Ferry lay just ahead on the Edisto. There would be food there at an old friend of the colonel's.

Mounting up, Jack pressed on, pausing often to listen. In the heavy fog every sound was amplified, and even the mooing of a cow sounded close.

Soon the dark shape of a house appeared through the mist. It was one of the many former slave houses that lined the entrance to the village of Parker's Ferry. In the yard of one of them a man was splitting wood. He straightened up to watch Jack's approach.

"G' mawning!" he called out in cheerful greeting. "Kinda foggy t' be a ridin', ain't it? A man could end up in one them inlets."

"Right you are, friend," Jack replied, pausing at the gate, "but give a good horse his head, and he'll get you there."

"Yes," the man answered, eyeing Prince with open admiration, "and that's sho' some horse."

"Prince will do to ride any trail with," Jack responded, giving the big horse a pat. He studied the man's aging black face for a moment, then asked, "What name do you go by?"

"Sam'el, suh, but I'm mostly known as Sam."

"Come here, Sam—I want to ask you something confidential," Jack said, beckoning the man to draw near.

A quizzical, guarded expression came over Sam's face as he complied. Surveying the surrounding area, Jack lowered his voice.

"Have you seen a young man go by here?"

"Who wants t' know?"

"My name is Captain Jack Brevard, and I saved this young man from a lynch mob last night. His name is Jess, and I'm hoping he'll make it to safety. If he comes through here, he may need your help."

"I don' know, Cap'n—I got my own troubles; nobody don' wanna be messin' with no lynch mob," Sam answered with a disturbed glance over his shoulder toward the house.

"He'll be coming to hunt me up in Charleston," Jack persisted. "All he'll need is a little rest and something to eat. Surely someone along here can do that."

"We'll see, Cap'n," Sam responded, turning away with a shrug of his shoulders. "Good day t' ya, suh."

Jack nudged Prince into a trot, reining in moments later before a large frame house at the edge of the Edisto River. Like most homes in the area, it was built high off the ground with a wide porch reaching around the sides, affording an excellent view of the river. Sliding stiffly from the saddle, he mounted the steps to cross the wooden floor, spurs jingling. At his knock a servant opened the door.

"Is Sanford Ravenswood in?" Jack inquired.

"Who should I say's a callin'?"

"Captain Jack Brevard, one of Colonel Stothard's men."

"Jackson Brevard! Is that you?" came a deep booming voice from within, followed by a thump, thump, thump. "Come in, man! Come in!"

Anxious to get in out of the dampness, Jack stepped into the big hall. Coming toward him, with his wooden leg pounding the floor, was Sanford Ravenswood.

"Abraham, tell that woman of yers to put another plate at the table. You will stay, Jack?"

"Be happy to, if it's not too much trouble."

"'Trouble,' he says! No trouble at all."

Ravenswood led him into the drawing room, where there was a welcome fire in the hearth. Jack stood before it a moment, then took the chair proffered him.

"Fire feels good today," his host commented. "Seemed like that storm left a chill in the air. Reckon we may have some winter soon—'n' these ol' bones cain't stand too much cold no more."

Jack studied the man's face as he poked at the fire, trying to push a log back. Ravenswood had aged since he had last seen him several years ago. His once-dark hair was now snow white, and his angular, good-natured face seemed hollow-cheeked.

"How's it going, Mr. Ravenswood?" Jack found himself asking.

"Abraham, fix this fire!" Ravenswood exclaimed with exasperation, giving up his own effort. "Tolerable well, Captain—jest tolerable. In weather like this, my game stump gets to achin'." Ravenswood referred to the leg he had lost to cannon shot in the war.

Dropping heavily into a chair facing Jack, he gave him a searching look.

"What brings ya into these parts, Captain? Everything's fine with the colonel and his missus, I hope."

"They're enjoying good health. I've never seen the colonel happier. He's thinking about running for the legislature."

"Now that's news!" Ravenswood exclaimed, slapping his good knee with his hand. "Be a good man fer the job. We need level-headed men like him in the restoration of the South—men who've a real interest in the people and the rebuildin' of our industrial base, instead of linin' their pockets."

Both men fell silent, and Ravenswood studied his companion's bearded face with serious gray eyes. Captain Jack was everything he admired in a man. Recalling the first time he had ever set eyes on him, he remembered the day Jack came riding into their camp to report for duty. His record had been as impeccable as his attire. His manner indicated he had come from a good family. Assigned to Colonel Stothard's command, Jack had risked his life to save him after his leg had been destroyed. Jack had possessed a sort of brave recklessness that Ravenswood had attributed to his youth, but after the beating death of young Jim Brevard, he was not sure. Older now, but still tall and round-limbed, Jack Brevard would turn any woman's head with his strong, angular face framed with black hair. Friendly eyes gazed at him now, but he had seen them turn to blue steel in threatening circumstances.

"What brings ya up this way, son?" Ravenswood asked, taking in Jack's tired, sleepless appearance. "I take it yer not just out fer a ride."

Jack waited until Abraham had finished replenishing the fire and was gone from the room before replying.

"Remember big Tom Searles?"

"That I do."

"I heard from him a few days ago." Jack took the letter from his pocket and handed it to Ravenswood.

After reading the rumpled page, Ravenswood sat staring gravely at the fire. His face took on a sadness that could not go unnoticed. The letter opened old wounds and stirred memories long pushed aside. So Searles *did* make it through Perryville Prison alive and was now living in the Charleston area. None of them had ever thought they would see him again. Tom Searles always had a knack for getting into trouble, and Perryville had dealt harshly with his kind. But what a soldier he had been!

Clemson? Strange he had not come in contact with the man if he was in the area, unless Clemson knew of his presence and avoided using the ferry. Of course, stove up like he was so often these days, he was not always on the job, Ravenswood admitted to himself, brushing a hand wearily across his face. Remembering his guest, he handed the letter back to Jack, who sat respectfully waiting.

"What do ya aim to do, son?" he queried.

"Pay an old debt," Jack responded with cold candor, his eyes becoming flintlike. "I want Clemson to beg for mercy like Jim did."

"I see," Ravenswood drawled with a deep sigh. "The war was awful, Jack, and we both did our share of killin'. But it's over. What yer thinkin' 'bout now will be murder. It's best ya let it lay. Besides, the Lord says, 'Vengeance is mine—I'll repay.' If Clemson is up to no good, let his Maker take care of 'im."

Jack got up and strode to the window. The colonel had given him similar advice. Seemed like the whole lot had gotten religion and were preaching at him.

His father had been like that, trying to cram it down his throat. Even while their home was being destroyed by the Union forces as they marched through Georgia, his father had held to his faith. The loss had proved too much, and he died of a stroke. Jim, his younger brother, had prayed every night, but where had it gotten him? Loss of her home and her husband had been hard on his mother, but when word of his brother's murder had come, she had died of a broken heart. Because of Clemson, his escape from prison had been thwarted, and he could not even be there to comfort her. Jack felt the old bitterness well up in him, and he stood looking out the window with clenched fists.

Neither man spoke for a long moment, and the silence between them was full. A knock at the outer door claimed the older man's attention, saving Jack a reply.

A lilting contralto voice could be heard talking to Abraham; then footsteps headed their way. He turned to see a golden-haired young lady burst through the door and rush over to

Ravenswood's side. Another young woman, of extraordinary beauty, followed to just inside the door, hesitant to proceed farther. Jack noted with aloof amusement that neither seemed to notice his presence.

"Uncle Sandy, Abraham said you were busy, but I know you can't be so busy you wouldn't want to see me—now would you, dear?" The blond girl pretended to pout, kissing him on the cheek.

"That I wouldn't, Tamara Sue," he returned fondly. "But who's the young lady ya have with ya?"

"Uncle Sandy, I want you to meet my best friend, Cordelia Dureen," she exclaimed, going to take the other girl by the hand to pull her forward. "Her brother is developin' land north of here, and I talked her into comin' on this trip with me."

"Any friend of my niece is welcome," Ravenswood boomed, getting to his feet to take gallantly the hand Cordelia held out to him.

The movement revealed Jack standing in the background staring at Cordelia. Surprise registered in her violet eyes—and something else—before she returned her gaze to acknowledge Ravenswood's greeting.

"Thank you, Mr. Ravenswood. It's a pleasure to meet you. Tamara has talked so much about you."

"All good, I trust," Ravenswood laughed. "Ya never know what Tammy Sue'll be tellin'. You'll stay fer dinner?"

"I'm glad you asked, Uncle Sandy—I'm famished; must've been the long ride out here," Tammy Sue answered, sniffing the air. "Sumthin' Cressie's cookin' sure smells good!"

Ravenswood suddenly exclaimed, remembering Jack's presence, "Where's my manners? Ladies, meet Captain Andrew Jackson Brevard. We fought in the war together. Jack, this is my niece Tamara Sue Sotherland and her friend Miss Cordelia . . ."

"Dureen," Tammy Sue reminded him.

"Ladies," Jack murmured, bowing slightly.

Both girls looked him over with more than a little interest, making him keenly aware of his rumpled clothes and unshaven appearance. Ravenswood's niece stepped forward to offer her hand. Her frank, wide-set hazel eyes were warm and friendly. He could see a dusting of freckles across the bridge of her nose.

"Please t' meet 'cha, Captain Andrew Jackson Brevard," she said, smiling up at him. "That's a mighty long name. What do your friends call you?"

"Most call me Jack," he replied quietly, taking her small hand in his.

Over her head his questioning gaze returned to Cordelia Dureen, who stood where she was, watching the two of them with an unfathomable expression, lips parted in a smile, revealing an even row of white teeth. Her violet eyes raised to meet his, and Jack felt something stir within him.

"Jack it is. Well, now, we girls will let you two get back to your important business," Tammy Sue drawled, turning to take Cordelia by the arm. "Come on, Cordie—let's go see if Cressie has some of her famous cookies! I've got to have somethin' to hold me over 'til dinner!"

"Send Abraham in, Tammy Sue," Ravenswood called after her, then sat drumming his fingers. Jack was glad the earlier conversation was being dropped and refrained from further comment.

"Abraham, show Captain Brevard to a room where he can rest and freshen up before dinner," Ravenswood instructed Abraham.

"I need to see to my horse first," Jack interposed. "He hasn't been fed or watered yet today."

"Never mind—Abraham will get the stable boy to see to it," Ravenswood added with a wave of his hand.

"Abraham, tell the boy that Prince doesn't take kindly to strangers," Jack warned, following him out, "and he mustn't try to ride him. Tell him to lead him by the bridle."

"Yes suh—I'll tell him," Abraham responded, nodding his gray head. "This way, suh."

Jack was shown to a room on the second floor. Abraham told him he would bring his things up to him. While he waited,

Jack sat down on the four-poster bed and surveyed the comfortable room with its simple furnishings. Besides a rocking chair, there was a commode bearing a large washbowl and pitcher, and a chifforobe. Walking to the window, he found himself looking down onto the stable area below. Beyond that was an impressive view of the Edisto River.

The stable boy came into sight, leading Prince into an open area with a roof over it. Jack watched as he removed the saddle and gave Prince a bucket of feed. While the big horse munched his oats, the boy brushed his coat until it glistened.

"Better be careful, Prince, ol' boy—a little of that kind of treatment can spoil you," Jack murmured out loud, turning away from the window. Removing his boots, he stretched out on the bed and fell asleep.

Jolted awake when Abraham shook him, Jack was stunned by the realization he had not even heard the man come into the room. He sat up on the side of the bed, trying to get his bearings.

"Dinner will be suhved in a little, suh," Abraham said, pouring water into the bowl. He laid out a towel and left the room. Jack dashed the cold water on his face and felt better. Looking around, he noted Abraham had brought his saddlebags while he slept, placing them on the chair. Twice the man had entered the room, and he had been too exhausted to detect his presence. Jack frowned at this prospect. Always a light sleeper, it was not like him to be unaware of what was going on around him. He would have to be more careful. A man with enemies could not afford to let down his guard, he thought grimly.

He took out his razor and a clean shirt, making quick work of changing his travel-worn appearance. Following the sound of voices, he found the others already in the dining room.

"Ah, there ya are!" his host greeted him cheerfully. "Sit right here, Jack. I trust ya got a little rest?"

"Some," Jack acknowledged, taking the seat indicated.

He found himself directly across from Cordelia Dureen, lovely in a blue dress that accented the whiteness of her skin and made her eyes luminous. His heart skipped a beat as she smiled in welcome.

"Well, it's mighty good to have some young folk around the table!" Ravenswood announced, as Cressie and Abraham brought in steaming bowls of food. "A body gets tired of eatin' to himself."

"In that case, we oughta come more often, Uncle Sandy," Tammy Sue commented. Turning to Cordelia, she continued, "When you taste Cressie's fried chicken and pecan pie, you'll agree, Cordie."

Jack filled his plate and gave his attention to eating, after the manner of a hungry man who had not eaten for a while. He did not realize how fast he was eating until he looked up to see Cordelia watching him with amusement. Laying his fork down, he took up his cup, pretending not to notice.

"Abraham tells me that's quite a hoss ya got, Jack," Ravenswood remarked, helping himself to another piece of chicken. "I take it he's probably one of the colonel's thoroughbreds."

"Name's Prince. He was sired by King, the colonel's prize stallion. He can outrun King, but the colonel wouldn't believe it. He gave him to me as a present when I left. I trained him, and he said I had ruined him for anyone else to ride. But I suspect he was afraid Prince would outrun King." Jack finished with a chuckle.

"You oughta see Cordelia's horse, Bangles," Tammy Sue said. "He's fast—and it's a sight to see her ride like the wind."

"Tammy Sue, how you do go on!" Cordelia scolded gently with heightened color. She looked over at Jack. "I'm afraid Tammy Sue is exaggerating."

"Do ya live around here, Miss Dureen?" Ravenswood asked.

"Right now she's visitin' me," Tammy Sue broke in before Cordelia could answer. "She's been stayin' with her brother. You should see the big house he's built—it's b-e-a-u-t-i-f-u-l! Bet you've never seen anything like it, Uncle Sandy!"

Cressie came in with a tray of pecan pie, and Tammy Sue squealed with delight.

"Ya'll ain't nevah ate anything like Cressie's pecan pie," Tammy Sue bragged. "Your stomach's gonna think you died and went to heaven!"

This brought laughter from the whole group and a broad smile from Cressie.

After Jack finished the last bite of his pie, he pushed back his plate. "I'm afraid I tend to agree with you, Miss Sotherland. My stomach was right pleased to receive Cressie's pecan pie."

"See, I told you," Tammy Sue stated triumphantly.

Jack got to his feet, glancing around the group. "If you folks will excuse me, I must be on my way," he said. "Sandy, I appreciate your kindness."

"So soon?" Ravenswood protested. "Won't hear of it! Why don't ya stay over, Jack? You and your horse both need the rest."

Remembering the comfortable bed upstairs, Jack hesitated, glancing down at Cordelia Dureen's upturned face. It had been a long time since he had been in such delightful company.

"If it won't be too much trouble," he heard himself saying, pleased at the glimmer he detected in Cordelia's eyes before she lowered her gaze. "I could sure use some rest. Been in the saddle a long time."

"Good!" Ravenswood exclaimed, spreading his hands on the table to raise himself out of his chair. "Now, let's take a look at this 'some kind o' hoss,' as Abraham put it."

"Do you mind if we come along?" Tammy Sue asked. "I'd like to see this 'some kind o' hoss' too. Wouldn't you, Cordie?"

Cordelia's murmured reply was lost in the thumping noise of Ravenswood's wooden leg as he and Tammy Sue led the way out the back, leaving Jack and Cordelia to follow. Ravenswood called to the stable hand, and he led Prince out. Jack whistled, and the stallion tossed his proud head, breaking free to trot over to him.

"Oh, you beautiful creature!" Cordelia cried with delight, throwing her arms around Prince's neck.

"Steady, boy," Jack commanded, grabbing for the halter. The horse had never been near a woman before, and Jack was not sure how he would react. He needn't have worried, though, for Prince seemed to respond to her soft touch. Jack could not keep his eyes off her radiant face as she stroked the stallion's forehead.

Ravenswood seemed almost speechless, pacing from side to side in open admiration. "Now I know what Abraham meant—I believe this is the finest hoss I've ever seen," he managed finally. "You may have a hard time holdin' on to him. There's plenty of men out there who'd want to steal a hoss like that!"

"That's already been tried," Jack said, looking around to see that the girls had wandered off toward the house. Turning Prince over to the stable hand, he drew Ravenswood out of earshot to tell him what had happened the night before. Ravenswood shook his head in disbelief.

"Well, what do ya know? I've been hearin' bits 'n' pieces of things, Jack, but 'til now I haven't lent much credence to it. So there really *is* a vigilante group? Do ya know who's behind all this?"

"I have my suspicions; have you ever heard of a place called Clemdenin Hall?" Jack asked, watching his friend's eyes closely.

"Can't say I have, Jack," Ravenswood answered, shaking his head. "Why?"

"I thought you might have heard some of your hands talking about it."

"I see; guess I can't help ya there," Ravenswood said, starting for the house. "Let's get out of this dampness. Seems to chill a body clean through."

"How's your business doing, Sandy?" Jack asked, waiting until Ravenswood had thumped his way up the steps and paused to get his breath.

"It's doing tolerable right now. But word's out they're gonna build a bridge over the Edisto. That'll put me out of business."

"Wouldn't have to," Jack responded. "You could sell your boat and open an inn. With Cressie's fine cooking, you'd do right well, I'd think."

"Maybe so, Jack." Ravenswood seemed pleased with the idea. "In the meantime, let's see what those young ladies are up to."

≡ 3 ≡

RAVENSWOOD AND JACK found Tammy Sue and Cordelia seated on the front veranda, where they could see the ferry going back across the river.

"Jack, I believe we were deserted," Ravenswood teased.

"We knew we couldn't compete with that hoss," Tammy Sue retorted with a toss of her head. "A woman has to admit when she's beat."

"Well, I reckon there's no hoss that can hold a candle to the likes of you two," Ravenswood returned gallantly, lowering himself into the last remaining rocker and leaving Jack to sit on the small swing with Cordelia. Jack studied his host's face, wondering if he had done it on purpose, but Ravenswood's expression looked innocent enough. Squeezed in beside her, Jack found her presence very disturbing and steeled himself against it. This was not the time for him to be thinking of the likes of Cordelia Dureen.

Lingering there to enjoy the warmth of the late afternoon sun, the group whiled away the time. Long shadows began to creep across the ground as the sun sank lower in the sky, allowing the chill to have more effect. Frothy waves kicked up by the stiff breeze disturbed a large blue heron, which took to the air, soaring gracefully to a post on the dock.

"We'd better be goin' when the ferry comes back, Uncle Sandy—we've stayed far too late," Tammy Sue spoke up. "We'll have to hurry to get home before dark."

"Why don't ya stay over?" Ravenswood urged. "I've got plenty of room, and it'll be much safer fer ya to travel in the daylight. 'Sides, Captain Brevard's goin' that way in the mornin', and he can ride part way with ya."

"I guess I could be coaxed into stayin' for another piece of Cressie's pecan pie," Tammy Sue admitted with a giggle, looking at Cordelia. "What do you think, Cordie?"

"I guess it will be all right," Cordie agreed, biting her lip thoughtfully. "My brother is away on business and won't be back until tomorrow."

"Good—now that we've settled on it, why don't we all get into the house before we catch our death?" Ravenswood suggested, hoisting himself from the chair to lead the way. "Ahh— Abraham has already laid a fire," he said when inside. "Pull up a chair, folks. I'll have some refreshments brought in."

The remainder of the evening was spent in pleasant conversation, with Ravenswood and the young ladies doing most of the talking. Jack was content to listen, watching the firelight play on the contours of Cordelia's face as she talked.

During a lull in the conversation, she turned her gaze on him. "Captain, is your family from around here?"

Jack was never comfortable talking about himself, but he sensed they were all waiting for his answer. "No, Miss Dureen— we had a place east of Atlanta before the war," he said. He glanced at Sanford Ravenswood. "Of late, I have been living in Savannah."

"Do you have family, Captain?" she asked.

"No, ma'am," Jack responded stiffly, noting Ravenswood turn his brooding eyes upon him. After a brief hesitation, he went on: "My folks are gone, and I've never married."

He stood to his feet. "Now, if you folks will excuse me, I think I'll turn in. Good night!"

Cordelia watched him stalk from the room, wondering if she had offended him, then turned a questioning glance on Ravenswood.

"Ladies, I think I'll do the same, if you don't mind," Ravenswood announced hastily, to escape the questions sure to come.

"We don't mind, Uncle Sandy," Tammy Sue yawned. "Cordie and I are ready to go to bed too."

Long after her friend had fallen asleep, Cordelia lay awake thinking about Jack Brevard. Not since the untimely death of her husband in the war had she been around a man who intrigued and interested her. His bearing spoke of good family background; his speech was that of a gentleman.

Several times that evening she had looked over to catch his gaze upon her, and when their eyes had met, his had burned with a strange, scintillating light that had sent her pulse racing.

Yet she sensed an aloofness about him that both fascinated and puzzled her. The ever-present gun he had strapped to his hip had sent chills over her as it brushed against her on the swing. Could it be he was running from the law? Not very likely. Ravenswood seemed to have high regard for him. But still she had sensed a tension between them, and he had beat a hasty retreat tonight when he thought she was about to voice the question on her lips. Well, tomorrow she would make it a point to ask Sanford Ravenswood more about him, she vowed sleepily.

The smell of coffee awakened her before dawn the next morning, and she could hear the thumping sound of Tammy Sue's uncle moving through the hall. Slipping from beneath the covers so as not to awaken Tammy Sue, Cordelia quickly dressed and made her way toward the kitchen. There she found Ravenswood sitting at a small table near the fire, enjoying a cup of coffee.

"Good mornin', lass. I see yer up early! Could it be ya smelled Cressie's coffee too? I trust ya slept well." Ravenswood's observant eyes studied her face.

"That I did, Mr. Ravenswood," she responded, taking a seat at the table across from him. "I'm an early riser. Morning is my favorite part of the day." Cressie came with a steaming cup of coffee, and Cordelia smiled her gratitude. "None of the other guests are up, I see," she said.

"If ya mean Captain Brevard," her host replied, giving her a searching look, "normally he would be, but he ain't had much sleep the last few days."

"You've known him a long time?" she asked, studying his face. "What kind of a man is he?"

"Jack Brevard is as straight as they come. Seen a lot of sorrow in his life, and it's left him a driven man. But they don't come any better than Jack."

"Does he always wear that gun?"

"I've never seen him without one," Ravenswood admitted, giving her a keen glance.

"Is he in some kind of trouble?"

"Not that I know of, lass—but he's carryin' a big load, even fer him," Ravenswood answered with knitted brows. "Only the Lord in heaven knows what lays ahead fer him."

Drinking the last of his coffee, he got to his feet, and Cordelia knew the conversation was over. His last comment was very much on her mind as she returned to her room to find Tammy Sue up and about.

"Oh, there you are," she was greeted. "I wondered where you went to."

"I was having a cup of coffee with your uncle."

"Were you talkin' about Captain Brevard?"

"Tammy Sue, what are you implying?" Cordelia said crossly.

"I saw the way you were lookin' at each other. He sure is handsome. Now, Cordie, don't tell me you haven't noticed."

"A woman would have to be dead not to notice, Tammy Sue," Cordelia admitted, feeling the heat come into her face. "How about helping me pull the bed straight?"

Instead, Tammy Sue answered a knock at the door. "Breakfast is ready, Miss Tammy," Abraham announced.

Their host was waiting in an alcove, sitting at a round table overlooking the river.

"What a nice view!" Cordelia remarked, taking the chair offered her.

There was a soft, jingling step, and Jack came into the room, looking handsome and rested. She was pleased to see his eyes seek her out and smiled her response.

Cressie came with platters of eggs, ham, grits, and biscuits, while Abraham poured coffee.

Jack didn't join in the breakfast chatter, the heavy burden of what lay ahead settling upon him. The moment he stepped out of this haven of safety, he would need his wits about him. Cordelia noticed the change in him and pondered it in her heart. He seemed aloof and preoccupied, as if he had disassociated himself from the rest of them, staring off across the river as he ate. If Ravenswood took notice, he did not let on, keeping up a light-hearted exchange.

The time came for them to leave, and the girls hurried for their things while the men went to the front, where Prince and the carriage were waiting.

Cordelia glanced out the window to see the two men engaged in earnest conversation. Ravenswood began gesturing pointedly, and his face became flushed as he stepped closer to place a hand on Jack's shoulder. Jack stood facing her, left hand on the pommel of his saddle, listening to his friend with cold detachment.

"Are you comin'?" Tammy said from the doorway.

When they walked outside, the men's conversation ended abruptly. Ravenswood helped his niece into the carriage, leaving Jack to assist Cordelia.

"Thank you, Captain; it was good to meet you—perhaps we will meet again," she said hopefully, with questioning eyes.

"Miss Dureen, the pleasure was mine," he replied, touching the brim of his hat.

Walking to his horse, he was about to step into the saddle when Ravenswood laid a restraining hand on his arm. "Jack, remember what I said," he implored again, "'n' let it be!"

Jack stared off toward the waiting ferry, then looked over at Cordelia and back to Sanford Ravenswood. "Thanks, Sandy—I'll keep it in mind," he answered stiffly, urging Prince into a trot and leaving the girls to follow at will.

The words kept ringing in Cordelia's ears as she kept her eyes glued on the broad shoulders ahead. Mr. Ravenswood had said Captain Brevard was carrying a heavy load, even for him.

"Cordelia, you haven't heard a word I've been sayin'," Tammy Sue chided.

"I'm sorry, Tam," Cordelia admitted. "I was just thinking about something."

"You were thinkin' about what my uncle said, weren't you?" Tammy observed, turning serious hazel eyes on her friend.

Cordie nodded.

"I thought so. I was wonderin' on it too. What do you suppose it was all about?"

"I don't know, Tam."

"Are you in love with him?"

Cordelia rolled her eyes impatiently at Tammy Sue but remained silent. Inwardly she cringed at Tammy Sue's directness. She knew Jack was as attracted to her as she was to him. Yet his guard seemed to be holding her off. Was it another woman? No. He had made that clear. He must be on some sort of mission. Another woman would be easier to cope with than a man's sense of duty. She had learned that from her late husband, who had marched off to war on their wedding day.

"Well, he's in love with you," Tammy continued, undaunted at her silence. "He may not know it yet, but he is." She gave the horses a flip of the reins to urge them into a faster pace.

Up ahead, Captain Brevard had pulled up to wait for them. He sat tall and straight in the saddle, with the proud bearing of a military man. Man and horse seemed as one, sitting in the gold of the morning sunlight.

"I reckon I better keep my mind on my drivin'," Tammy giggled, as he turned Prince loose at a fast trot again. "It appears our escort is in somewhat of a rush."

Soon he dropped back to ride just ahead of the horses. What had dictated the change Cordelia had no way of knowing, but she was glad to have him closer.

When Tammy Sue pulled up at the place where they were to turn off, Jack rode up close. "How far do you have to go yet, Miss Sotherland?" he asked.

"It's not far, Captain," Tammy Sue replied. "Thank you for ridin' along with us."

"My pleasure," he returned with curt politeness. "Keep a sharp eye, and don't tarry along the way."

"Uncle Sandy has already warned us, Captain, but we're thankin' you anyway," Tammy Sue said soberly.

"Times being what they are, it isn't safe for you ladies to be out alone," Jack continued, his gaze shifting to Cordelia. "You will be careful?"

"Yes, Captain, thank you," Cordelia responded warmly, reaching out a gloved hand to him.

At her touch, the change in him was profound. A fleeting look of gladness swept across his face to disappear at her next remark: "I trust the rest of your journey will be in peace."

She felt him stiffen, and the warmth in his eyes was replaced by a coldness that startled her.

"Peace for me is an elusive dream, madam," he said bluntly, withdrawing his hand to touch the brim of his hat. "Good day." Turning Prince away, he galloped off.

The dark mood stayed with him for miles as he scolded himself over and over for bringing hurt to her eyes. He was glad when he came to the Ashley River. Across its wide expanse he could see the city of Charleston. Fortunately, the ferry was on his side and Prince thundered aboard. The pilot, a young towheaded man in his 20s, greeted him amiably, ogling the mighty horse.

Jack dismounted to stand and talk with him. He seemed a wealth of information about activities in the area, readily answering Jack's queries.

"Tell me—have you ever heard of a place called Clemdenin Hall?" Jack asked, abruptly changing the subject.

First surprise, then a guarded look registered on the fellow's face. "No suh, I ain't never heard of a place by that name," he declared, walking away.

Jack knew he was lying but let the moment pass. The boat was nearing the shore anyway. Mounting up, he rode over to where the fellow stood. "Which way to Legare Street?" he asked.

"Over thataway, Mista. Go down t' that first road there, 'n' foller it around."

"Thanks."

It was late in the afternoon when Jack rounded the corner of Legare Street, to be met with a brisk breeze off the waterfront. Finding the house answering the description in the letter, he reined in and tied Prince to the black iron hitching post. Looking up at the pretentious two-story dwelling with side porch on each floor, he whistled softly to himself.

"Well, Tom, seems like you've done pretty well by yourself," he muttered, unlatching the tall gate to enter a small courtyard leading to open-arm steps. A servant answered his knock, peeking at him through a four-inch crack.

"Is Mr. Thomas Searles in?"

"Who be it callin'?"

"Captain Jack Brevard. He's expecting me."

The door swung open to reveal a young woman. Her eyes widened slightly as she looked him over. He stepped inside the center hall, and she disappeared in the dim interior of the house. Some moments later, she returned to beckon him to follow her. He was led through the richly furnished house and out to a secluded corner of a small porch in the rear.

There he found Tom Searles sitting in a big batwing chair, legs up on a stool, covered with a blanket.

"Jack, my friend, it's good t' see you! Come, come—pull up a chair. Pardon me fer not gettin' up. I'm pretty stove up wi' these bad legs of mine—a souvenir from Perryville Prison."

Jack chose a wicker chair across from his host. Perryville had aged Thomas Searles, but the same dark eyes gazed at him. His large hulk filled the chair, and his enormous head was balding. He had gained some weight but still appeared muscular. His round face was amiable now, but Jack remembered it could be cold and heartless.

"Didn't know you were still alive, Tom, until I got your letter—seems like you're doing well," Jack answered the greeting, flipping a hand to indicate the house and the garden beyond.

"I'm gettin' by, Jack," Tom admitted. "Makin' a little on crops. By the way, have you eaten?"

"No, I came directly here," Jack explained. "I was delayed a little in my trip and thought you might be wondering if I was coming."

"No matter. We'll eat presently." Tom rang a bell by his chair, and the maid appeared instantly. Jack wondered if she had been hovering near the door.

"Mantie, bring our guest somethin' t' drink 'n' prepare enough food fer him. He'll be stayin' fer supper. What'll you have, Jack?"

"Coffee's fine."

When Mantie had returned with his drink, Jack approached the subject that brought him to Charleston.

"You said in your letter Clemson was here in the area?"

A guarded expression came over Tom's face, and he gave a warning glance toward the door. "We'll talk later. I make it a policy not t' talk when I could be overheard."

"So when did you get out of Perryville?" Jack asked, changing the subject.

"Not 'til the war was over. I thought I was goin' t' die in there. Jack, if you think we had it bad in Pulaski, it was worse than death in Perryville. T' survive, you lived like an animal, by your wits, 'n' sheer determination t' stay alive."

"Did you ever marry?"

"Oh yes, I met 'n' married a widow woman, not long after I got back t' Charleston. She died near a year ago—jest up 'n' died. That's how I got this place." Tom looked around with satisfaction. He reached for the bell and rang it. Mantie came running.

"Bring my chair—this dank's gettin' t' me," he ordered in a harsh voice. "The dew's beginnin' t' fall."

When Mantie reappeared, she was pushing a large chair with wheels. Bringing it close to his side, she tried to hold it steady until he had changed his seat. It was hard to do as he maneuvered his bulk into it, and Jack sprang to his feet to assist her.

"Leave 'er be, Jack—she don't need no help. She does this all the time. Ain't that right, Mantie?"

"Yes, suh—I doin' all right, suh," Mantie asserted with something akin to fear in her eyes.

Jack watched helplessly as she strained to push Tom's weight into the house. Struggling with the door sill, she pushed with all her might. Unseen by Tom, Jack aided her with the toe of his boot, receiving a grateful glance.

Inside, Tom was wheeled into the dining room and left at the end of the table. Jack followed, taking the chair Tom indicated. The big man sat there drumming his fingers. Jack sensed Mantie would be in trouble if she didn't get the food in a hurry. Tom must have read his thoughts, for he said, "Prison changes a man, Jack. I guess I have little patience left. If I seem crude t' ya, I only ask yer forbearance."

Mantie came into the room with a large tray laden with steaming bowls of food, giving him no occasion to answer. Both ate in silence as she tended to their needs. Tom picked food from the plate with his fingers, making Jack grateful he had taken all he wanted the first time around. When Tom saucered his coffee and drank it with a loud sucking noise, Jack kept his eyes glued to his plate.

Tom cleared his throat noisily and asked Mantie to bring the dessert. When she offered him some, he rudely waved it aside, grabbing another piece of chicken instead. Jack accepted the warm slice of pecan pie Mantie held out to him.

"This is only the second good meal I've had in many days, Mantie—thank you," he remarked, looking up at her. A fleeting, puzzled expression came into her eyes and vanished, causing him to wonder. He thought of Jess, but a sixth sense restrained him from asking Searles if he had shown up.

"Mantie, when you're through wi' yer chores, ya can go t' yer room," Tom instructed tersely. "Mind ya, be up early in the mornin'. I've got a lot of business t' tend t'."

"Yes suh—I be up," Mantie responded, clearing the plates away.

"Now, Jack, if you'll jest roll me into the drawin' room, we'll have a talk."

When they arrived in the designated room, Jack went back to pull the double doors shut as big Tom transferred his hulk into his favorite chair before the fire. Standing with his arm resting on the mantel, he waited for Tom to speak.

"There's some brandy there in the cabinet, if you've a mind t' have some, Jack."

"No, thanks. I'm not a drinking man."

"Ah—that fire feels good. Been havin' a cool spell after that rain."

Jack pondered this comment. If he wasn't mistaken, it had not rained here in the Charleston area for quite a while. Things were looking pretty dry.

"Been having quite a bit of rain, have you?" he asked innocently enough.

"A band of showers went by several days ago," Tom answered, taking a cigar from a box by his side. Striking a match to it, he sent clouds of smoke toward the ceiling, then flipped the match into the fire, giving Jack a shrewd look. "We didn't get any of it here, but one of my field workers reported a torrent south of here. Ya must've run into it."

"Ran into some fog," Jack admitted, giving no hint of his wariness. "Stopped off to see a friend on the way up."

He had known Tom Searles a long time, fought beside him in the war, served time in a Union prison with him. But that had been a long time ago.

A timid knock came at the door. "Did ya need anythin' more, suh?"

"I told ya—go t' yer room," Searles said harshly.

Jack averted his eyes to hide the glint of anger that appeared at Searles's treatment of the girl. Looking through the window, he could see an old man making his way wearily up the street in the dusk.

"Ya asked about Clemson," Tom was saying when Jack turned his attention back into the room. "I hear tell he's built him a big place on some good land south of here. Don't know where he got all his money, unless it was from squealin' on us. The other day I even heard he was thinkin' of runnin' fer the legislature. Now, I don't know about ya'll, Jack, but I ain't about t' be governed by no carpetbaggin' traitor. I reckoned it was about time we took care of him."

Tom's gruffness stirred something in Jack's memory. The image of a shadowy figure on a horse came to mind. No, couldn't be. Tom didn't look as though he could even sit on a horse. Darkness was coming on, and Jack left the window to take a seat facing Searles.

"Do you have a plan?" Jack asked quietly.

"Been thinkin' on it a long time, Jack, as you probably have too, 'n' it's been eatin' on me. I jest thought this was the time t' take care of the problem so we can live the rest of our lives in peace, knowin' the score was settled."

Encouraged by Jack's nod, Tom warned, "It ain't gonna be easy. He's flyin' high these days, 'n' there's always people, especially women, around. Anyway, I figured ya bein' such a good shot with a rifle, ya could watch until the time's right 'n' pick him off out in some lonely place."

Searles shifted his heavy weight in the chair and pulled the cover straight over his legs. "I'd do it myself, Jack, if it wasn't fer these bum legs. I never thought the day would come when big Tom Searles would be hog-tied t' a chair," he finished, covering his face with his gnarled hands.

Jack felt a sense of pity for the man. It had not been easy for either of them, but Tom had gotten the worst of it, he thought.

"I'm sorry, Tom. I want you to know that it hurts me to see you like this. You're probably tired, and I must go. We'll talk again in a day or so. In the meantime, I want to take a look around and learn some things. I see no need to hurry this thing. I'll be choosing my own time."

"Fine with me. You'll stay the night?"

"I'd best get a room somewhere," Jack answered, getting to his feet. "It wouldn't be good for me to be seen hanging around here. Thanks for the offer." He headed for the door. "Where did Mantie put my hat?"

"Probably on the rack there by the door. When will ya be back?"

"Three days from now, after dark, about this time."

"I'll be anxious t' hear what you've uncovered," Tom called after him, his tone more cheerful. "Good night!"

*J*ACK STEPPED INTO THE SADDLE and slowly rode away, turning east to King Street, which led toward the center of town. There he knew he would find an inn with a good stable for Prince. He had stayed there before and appreciated the fact it had a back staircase as well as one leading up from the lobby.

Once settled in, Jack removed his boots and stretched out on the bed. He needed time to think over the happenings of the last couple of days. If Jess had made it, there was no mention of it by Tom Searles or his maid, Mantie. Remembering the look of fear in her eyes and Tom's obvious disdain, Jack was glad he had not approached the subject with Searles.

His mind went back to Searles. The plot he had laid out did not appeal to Jack. He had never been one to shoot a man in the back, even in the war, and he would not do it now, no matter how much he hated him. A sense of fairness had always dictated giving the enemy an equal chance to live or die.

The words of Colonel Stothard and Sanford Ravenswood came back to him: "What you're thinking about now is murder." It would not be murder if he gave Clemson a fair chance, he reasoned to himself.

Tomorrow he would take a look around the countryside and ask questions. Perhaps a ride out to Dreyton Hall would be a good start. John Dreyton was about his own age, and though they had fought on different sides in the war, they had remained friends. Dreyton would be a reliable source of information.

A fair face penetrated his thoughts. With her dark hair and fair skin, Cordelia Dureen was a most beautiful woman, but with an inner beauty and grace much like his mother's. When all this was over, and he lived through it . . . perhaps . . .

"What makes you think she would have anything to do with a murderer?" a voice in his head accused.

Not since the war had he fired his weapon at another human being with the intent to kill. The colonel had inspired his men to use their heads to avoid violence.

Jack sprang from the bed to walk the floor. Why all these troubling thoughts had come to him he did not know. Maybe he was getting older and things appeared different to him now. Maybe he was lonely. All the colonel's men had married and settled down except him. Though they had teased him about not finding the right woman, they all knew the bitterness he carried deep inside.

Hanging his gun belt on the bedpost, Jack shed his clothes, blew out the lamp, and slipped between the covers. Though weary in body, his thoughts wandered back to Cordelia Dureen. Her face with dark, luminous eyes smiled at him in the dark. He wondered if she was thinking of him. Probably not, he thought, thoroughly disgusted with himself. A woman such as she would have many admirers, and he would be but one more. Pounding his pillow harder than necessary to fluff it, he turned over and went promptly into a troubled sleep in which her presence was always just beyond his grasp.

* * *

Cordelia Dureen surveyed her wardrobe. She had been invited to Dreyton Hall for an overnight stay. John and Martha Dreyton were having guests and wanted her to join the party. Although she knew they always invited her when they were having eligible bachelors, she did not mind, for they were gracious hosts, and she enjoyed their company.

"Hettie, you may pack the white gown for the party, and I'll travel in the blue velvet," she instructed the maid standing next to her. "Be sure to put in all the other things I'll need: my jewelry, gloves, and all."

"I'll take care of it real fine, Miss Cordelia, 'n' I won't be forgettin' nothin'," Hettie responded with a broad smile. She looked forward to Miss Cordelia going to Dreyton Hall, for she usually accompanied her. It wasn't "fittin'" for a fine lady like Miss Cordelia to travel alone, and it wasn't uncommon for a lady to bring her maid to help her dress. She laid out the things Miss Cordelia needed, then went downstairs to get a small traveling trunk.

Cordelia removed the pins from her hair and went to the mirror to give it a good brushing before retiring. Staring at her image in the mirror, her thoughts went to Captain Jack Brevard, and she tried to analyze what it was about him that had attracted her. Certainly it wasn't his attire, for his rumpled clothing held none of the signs of wealth. It was his virile strength and gentle manner, she decided. Yet in spite of the warmth she had seen in his eyes, there was something detached and unapproachable about him that troubled her. Well, it wasn't likely she would see him again anyway, she thought, dismissing him from her mind.

The next morning the fog had given way to bright sunlight. Cordelia was grateful for its warmth. The ride in from the lowlands was pleasant, and when the driver slowed the carriage to pass between the pillared gate into the broad drive leading back to Dreyton Hall, she felt a sense of anticipation. She had always loved this old homeplace nestled in the trees on the banks of the Ashley River. It had survived terrible storms, the Civil War, and the greatest enemy—fire, which had claimed many of the old estates built by the sturdy pioneers who had settled the area. This one had seen many generations of the Dreytons.

The road wound through the fields, past the former slave cabins and storage buildings, to a wide, columned veranda across the rear of the house. The main entrance faced the river, where most guests coming by boat from Charleston were received.

A hired hand came running to help with the luggage. Cordelia and Hettie were greeted by one of the servants, who led them into the house. Martha Dreyton came hurrying toward them.

"Cordelia! We're delighted ya'll could come! Hettie, it's good to see ya again!"

Taking Cordelia by the hand, Martha led her into the sitting room. Two tall figures got to their feet, but Cordelia had eyes for only one.

"John, Cordelia is here."

"Cordelia, so glad you could come! I want you to meet an old friend of mine, Captain Jack Brevard. He's payin' us a surprise visit. I've been tryin' to get him to stay for the evenin' and meet my guests."

"The captain and I have met, John. It is good to see you again, Captain Brevard," Cordelia said cordially, smiling up at him.

Accepting the small hand she offered, Jack bowed, feeling very much like a drowning man. The same face haunting him in his sleep was looking up at him now, waiting for him to speak.

"Well, I do declare," Dreyton drawled, breaking the silence. "I had no idea you two had ever met."

"It seems the captain and I have some friends in common," Cordelia murmured softly, withdrawing her hand.

"That bein' the case, you two will have things to talk about. Jack, you will stay?"

"I didn't bring appropriate clothing, John."

"Nonsense—you and I are about the same size. Take what you need from my wardrobe. I'll have your boots polished and ready."

"In that case, I can't refuse," Jack replied, tearing his gaze away from Cordelia's face.

"Your brother isn't goin' to make it?" Dreyton asked, turning to Cordelia.

"He said to tell you he would very much like to be here, but he had some urgent business demanding his immediate attention," Cordelia explained. "He's been working so hard, and it seems there's never an end to trouble these days."

"Trouble? What kind of trouble?" Dreyton pressed, giving her a keen glance.

"I'm not sure," Cordelia replied, wrinkling her brow. "My brother rarely confides in me."

"This is no time or place for such talk," Martha Dreyton interrupted, drawing Cordelia toward the door. "We ladies have more pleasant things to think about."

After the women were gone, Dreyton went to a small cabinet and pulled out a bottle.

"Will you join me in a touch of brandy?"

"No, thanks. I never developed a taste for the stuff. Besides, in my line of work one has to have a clear head."

Dreyton poured himself a small glass of the liquor and settled his lithe figure into a chair. Brown hair, graying a little at the temples, framed a finely chiseled face. Immaculately dressed in gray trousers tucked into black, shiny boots, and wearing a light gray shirt, John Dreyton looked every inch the country gentleman.

Studying his guest with shrewd eyes, he asked, "What's your line of work, Jack?"

Jack thought about the question for a moment with furrowed brow. What *was* his line of work? He had always stood for right against wrong. Until recently he had been on the colonel's payroll. But now he was out of a job.

"I guess you would call me a defender of people."

"I see—you're a law officer. What brings you up in this area? Are you lookin' for somebody?"

"John, have you ever heard of Clemdenin Hall?"

"Only once. I overheard one of the men workin' for me whisperin' it to another worker. When I asked him about it, he clammed up and refused to say any more. But I could tell the name struck fear in him. What do you make of it?"

"They have a very real reason to be afraid of the name," Jack replied, deciding to take Dreyton into his confidence. Jack proceeded to tell of his encounter with Jess and the would-be vigilantes. His host leaned forward in his chair, hanging on every word.

"I'd say you had a close call, my friend!" Dreyton exclaimed, expelling a long breath. "I've heard rumors of such things, but no one knew for sure."

"John, do you know anything of what Miss Dureen hinted at?"

"Some of the planters have complained of crops bein' ruined and bales of cotton bein' stolen. One man had his whole rice field destroyed, but there's been no investigation into the matter. Some have lost their land as a result of lost crops, mostly among the Blacks. Many planters have put that down to lack of business skills. But I don't know," Dreyton concluded, setting his glass down. "I kinda doubt that. These people are hard workers, and they sure have the incentive to succeed if left alone." He got to his feet and walked to the window to look out.

"Jack, we planters close to Charleston are so far from the low country and tidal basins, it's hard for us to know what's goin' on down there. The folks at Magnolia and Boone Hall don't know any more than I do. What we hear is mostly at the market when the crops are bein' brought in. And that's from the Whites. The Blacks are afraid to talk, except among themselves. Little wonder, after listenin' to your story."

Dreyton turned from the window to look at Jack. "But that's not why you're here, is it?"

"Partly."

"You're lookin' for someone, aren't you, Jack?"

"I'm trying to find someone I knew a long time ago," Jack replied evasively. "I heard he may be in this area."

"What can I do to help you?"

"Tell me who will be my friends."

They talked on for more than an hour. Jack listened carefully while Dreyton talked of the people in the area and incidents that might be of interest. The sun was getting low in the sky when Dreyton suggested they had better check on a change of apparel for Jack. He called for a servant, who appeared immediately.

"Yes suh, Mista John?"

"George, our guests will be arrivin' soon, and I need to greet them. I hear the boat comin' now. Please take Captain Brevard to a room and find him a change of clothin' for dinner. Whatever he needs, get it for him, and see to havin' his boots polished."

"You're in good hands, Jack," Dreyton said, shrugging into a black pinstripe coat.

Upstairs, Jack found George very amiable help. He seemed to know just what would look good on Jack and laid it out for him. Jack studied the face before him as he removed his boots, careful to slip a small revolver from the side of one of them.

"George, you've worked for Mr. Dreyton a long time?"

"Yes suh, Cap'n, a long time," George replied, exposing two rows of white teeth. "I was born here at Dreyton Hall 'n' lived here all my life. My pappy worked fer Mista John's pappy."

"But you're free now. Haven't you ever wanted to leave, to have a place of your own?"

"No suh, Cap'n. This is my home. I'm happy here. My family is happy 'n' safe here. We love Mista John 'n' Miss Martha. They pay me real good. We're fam'ly."

"George, have you ever heard of Clemdenin Hall?" Jack asked unexpectedly.

George was pouring water into a large basin on the washstand. He stiffened perceptibly, then went on pouring, setting the pitcher down before he turned to face Jack. All friendliness had left his countenance, and his eyes were guarded.

"Why ya askin', Cap'n?"

"Because I am concerned about a friend. His name is Jess. I saved him from a lynch mob a few nights ago and told him to meet me somewhere. He hasn't shown up, and I'm worried about him."

"No suh, I ain't never heared of that place, Cap'n—no suh," George stated emphatically, wagging his craggy gray head back and forth in denial.

Knowing the man was not telling the truth, Jack felt it would be futile to pursue the matter further and changed the subject. "George, if I needed a friend among your people, who could I go to?"

George gave him a strange look, much the same as he had seen in Mantie's eyes. "Wha' kin 'my people,' as ya says, ever do fer you, Cap'n?"

"I don't rightly know, George. And I don't know who my enemy is. I hid Jess, and the vigilantes told me if I found him to take him to Clemdenin Hall. Seems no one knows of this place, if it is a place. After I helped Jess escape, they came back to burn me alive in Jess's father's homeplace. I had suspected they'd be back, so I hid out, slipping away to safety. But out there somewhere I have enemies, and I don't know who these people are."

"Word has it you was askin' 'bout young Jess. What ya want Jess fer?"

"I just want to know if he's safe," Jack explained. "When he didn't come to wait for me, I feared he didn't make it."

George gave him a penetrating look bordering on distrust, picked up Jack's boots, and turned to leave the room.

"George, wait! Send word to Jess that I need him. Tell him he can find me at the Charlestonian Inn in Charleston."

George gave no evidence he had heard as he walked out, closing the door. Jack scowled at the door. What was wrong around here? Shrugging his shoulders in a gesture of futility, he walked to the window. Down a wide, flower-bordered path he could see people alighting from a boat that had pulled up to the dock. John Dreyton came into sight and strode forward to greet them.

Jack lingered over his bath, taking great pains to shave and trim the beard he wore. Dreyton's black trousers fit him fine, but the snow-white shirt fit snugly, bearing testimony that Jack was more muscular. Slipping into the long coat, he studied himself in the mirror. Not bad for borrowed clothes, he thought.

Sounds of merry laughter floated up the open stairwell from the great hall below. Jack decided it was time to put in an appearance but remembered George had not returned with his boots. He wondered what was keeping him. While he waited, he folded his own clothing into a neat pile, arranging it in such a way that he would know if it had been disturbed, then placed his gun belt on top. That done, he sat down to wait for his boots.

He could hear the people downstairs moving into another part of the house. Impatience was building within him. Where was George? Getting to his feet, he strode to the door. Turning the knob, he opened it a crack to look out. The hall was empty, but his boots were sitting at his feet.

* * *

When Jack entered the dining room, the guests were being seated. Dreyton looked up from helping Martha with her chair.

"Oh, there you are, Jack. Ladies and gentlemen, I want you to meet a good friend of mine, Captain Jack Brevard. Jack, your seat is here." He indicated a chair opposite Cordelia Dureen, who was a vision in white satin and lace.

Cordelia smiled her greeting as he seated himself, but throughout the rest of the meal her attention was taken by the dapper middle-aged man with pasty skin seated on her right. Dismay and something akin to jealousy stirred deep within

Jack at first, but as he watched and listened, the feeling turned to amusement.

From the conversation, he gathered the man was a banker who, filled with a sense of self-importance, tried to impress Cordelia with talk of the many banking exploits he had successfully manipulated. Cordelia handled it gracefully but appeared grateful when the buxom lady on her left turned to make a comment. Her eyes met Jack's, and she blushed at his knowing glance.

Jack politely made small talk with those around him but was relieved when the meal was over. Dreyton invited his guests out onto the veranda for coffee. The evening was warmed by the slanting rays of a late sun, and everyone settled down comfortably, the men at one end and the women at the other. Jack chose to remain standing, leaning against one of the large columns for support. He listened attentively as the rest talked of planting, crops, and the market.

"John, did you hear what happened to poor George Medford?" the banker asked during a pause in the talk.

"Can't say I have, Wilford. What happened?"

"His whole cotton crop was destroyed by fire," Wilford Crenshaw stated, swelling up with importance. "I guess it's wiped him out. He came to me wanting to borrow more money, but I just couldn't let him have any more. Too bad. I like Medford, but business is business."

"What's he goin' to do?" Dreyton asked, leaning forward in his chair.

"I don't know," Crenshaw answered, warming up to the limelight. "He told me a fella came by and offered him cash for his land. But the price was so low he refused."

"Did he say who it was?"

"No. But he did mention the fellow was from Clemdenin Hall and told Medford that if he changed his mind to send word."

Dreyton gave Jack a startled glance, then lowered his eyes. Flicking an early mosquito that had landed on his knee, he shifted his position. When he spoke again, his tone was casual.

"Did he say where this Clemdenin Hall was?"

The men grew quiet, waiting for Crenshaw's answer.

"No, he didn't. If I remember correctly, I asked him, and he seemed puzzled. 'I'm not sure it's a place,' he says."

"Well, enough of this serious talk," Dreyton announced, getting to his feet. "Gentlemen, we wouldn't want the ladies to think we're neglectin' them, would we? I'll go see if all is in readiness."

The men went on to talk about things of little interest to Jack, who remained silent and thoughtful, turning Crenshaw's comment over and over in his mind.

In a matter of moments the strains of violins drifted on the night air. Couples began moving in the direction of the music. Crenshaw hurried to Cordelia's side to claim her for the first dance, while Jack stared morosely from the shadows.

Dancing had never been something he relished. Not that he was above the enjoyment of the company of a lovely lady; it was just that he felt awkward and ill at ease. Raised in a strictly religious home, he had not come in contact with this social event until the war. Even then he had avoided the officers' balls as much as possible.

Moving along with the rest, Jack stood to the side, watching the gliding couples. The table they had eaten from just shortly before had been pushed to one side and loaded with punch and delicacies. Just beyond were the musicians, a stringed quartet.

Chairs had been placed around the room against the wall, but Jack chose not to seek one out, preferring instead to stand in the shadows of the large mantel over the fireplace. From this vantage point, he could discreetly watch the waltzing couples. It did not take long for his eyes to seek out Cordelia Dureen. Crenshaw was an excellent dancer, and Cordelia appeared to be enjoying his company. This fact gave rise to another pang of jealousy.

Jack impatiently changed his position, disgusted with himself. What right did he have being jealous of this woman?

She was free to do as she pleased. At that moment he saw her look around the room as if searching for someone. Was it his imagination, or did her face lose some of its color as her eyes frantically searched the crowd?

Stepping out into the light so he could be seen, Jack was rewarded with a smile when she noticed the movement and saw him there. The effect on him was startling. His heart leaped within him, and he felt the blood pound in his temples. She had been looking for him!

"She's very beautiful, isn't she?" a voice said in his ear. Jack turned to find Dreyton standing beside him. How long had he been there?

"Wilford Crenshaw is crazy about her and wants to marry her," Dreyton went on, "but she has never given him any encouragement. He's a man of means and would be able to give her the things she's accustomed to havin'."

Jack remained silent, pondering the meaning behind Dreyton's remark.

"What did you make of Crenshaw's remarks earlier?" Dreyton asked when no comment was forthcoming.

"I'm not sure," Jack responded in a quiet voice. "It appears to be a land-grabbing operation. It's an old game. Search out those who are in trouble at the bank and dependent on the crops to bail them out, destroy the crops, then step in at the right time as benefactor to buy them out. But who?"

"You're surely not suggestin' Crenshaw is involved," Dreyton said sharply, giving Jack a hard look. "Wilford Crenshaw is a fine man, also very wealthy."

"I'm not suggesting anything, John," Jack returned bluntly. "You asked me what I thought, and I told you."

Cordelia and Crenshaw were close by when the music stopped, and they made their way toward them. "My, but you two look glum!" Cordelia observed.

"The captain and I were talkin' over some business," Dreyton informed her.

"Well in that case, maybe Captain Brevard needs to be rescued. You two have been talking 'business' all afternoon." She laughed.

"Are you implyin' Captain Brevard has the next dance?" teased Dreyton.

"If the captain would like," she replied modestly, turning a rapt gaze on Jack.

"Miss Dureen, may I have this dance?" Jack found himself saying as the music began again.

Taking her by the hand, he led her to the center of the room and went through the motions, moving her gracefully around the floor. Her nearness and the look in her eyes were disturbing. He steered her toward the door and out onto the veranda, where he released her.

"I'm sorry—I guess I'm not much of a dancer," he said in an unsteady voice.

"On the contrary, Captain, you are an excellent dancer," Cordelia declared appealingly.

"That's not what I mean. It's just—well, I don't enjoy dancing."

"I—I don't understand. What are you saying? You don't want to dance with me?"

"No—I mean yes—it's not that!"

For the first time in his life, Andrew Jackson Brevard found himself at a loss for words. Her nearness had a devastating effect on him. Though he had been a target of many a woman's conquest, he had treated them with respect, escaping their wiles. Never had a woman held such a power over him as this one. He turned to stare out into the darkness, embarrassed at acting like a schoolboy.

"Then what is it, Captain?" Cordelia whispered, plucking at his sleeve.

With a groan, he turned to her. She was lovely standing there in the dim light looking up at him. He could not see her eyes but felt their solemn gaze. To tell her anything but the truth did not occur to him.

"When I went off to war I made a promise to one I loved very much that I would not drink, smoke, or do anything to lead me down a wanton path. That person was my mother, and I have kept that promise since that day. The war took my father and my brother, and I was rotting in a Union prison when she died of a broken heart. My family were devout Christians. Dancing was not a part of our social life. Although I did not share their belief, I honored it. As an officer, there were times I had to attend the balls, so I learned to dance, but I am not comfortable with it."

He waited for her to speak. When she didn't, he led her back to the dance, where she was claimed promptly by Wilford Crenshaw. Making sure he was unobserved, Jack climbed the stairs to change his clothes. I was a fool to stay, he thought gloomily. When it came to the social life of the day, he was like a fish out of water. Once dressed, he looked around the room, picked up his hat and gun belt, and walked out. In the hall downstairs, he paused to strap on his gun.

"Leavin' so soon, Jack?" It was John Dreyton.

"I've got a lot of riding to do, John. I want to thank you for your hospitality."

"You are welcome, friend. You will keep in touch?"

Jack Brevard nodded and strode into the night. The stable boy led him to Prince's stall, and it took only moments for Jack to saddle up. Where he was going he had no idea, but he needed to think. And the only way he could think clearly was to get away from the presence of Cordelia Dureen.

*   *   *

When the music stopped, Cordelia was breathless. Sending Wilford Crenshaw for a cup of punch, she looked around the room for the familiar face. When she saw Dreyton walk in from the front door, she knew Jack Brevard was gone, and her heart sank. An eager Crenshaw returned with her drink, but she was no longer in a party mood. Excusing herself, she sought out Martha.

"Martha, dear, would you forgive me, please? I've come down with a dreadful headache. I think I'll go to my room and rest."

"Of course, dear. Go ahead. It's been a long day for ya. Can I get ya anything?"

"No, I'll be fine, thank you," Cordelia assured her, glad for the chance to escape the close scrutiny of her friend.

≡ *5* ≡

*J*ACK SET PRINCE AT A FAST PACE once he had cleared the stone entrance, turning south toward the Edisto. For answers he would have to find Jess.

Dawn found him haggard and tired at the edge of the river. Stepping wearily from the saddle, he raised the white flag used to signal the ferry that a customer was waiting. Jack watched as it slowly put out from shore, hoping Ravenswood was not aboard. He did not have time to visit. But he need not have worried, for it was much too early for the elderly man.

Chatting amiably with the pilot of the boat during the return crossing, Jack found him a well of information. A wizened, middle-aged man, he punctuated his words every now and then with a spat of tobacco juice into the clear green water alongside the boat. It seemed George Medford wasn't the only one who was mysteriously losing crops. Several planters had shared their woes with the ferryboat operator. Someone was wanting to get rich—very rich.

"Well, sir, thanks for the ride," Jack said when the boat reached the opposite shore. "It's been interesting to talk with you."

Jack gained his seat in the saddle. "By the way, have you ever heard of Clemdenin Hall?"

"Yes, sir, I heard one of the men mention it," the man answered, as he finished tying the mooring rope.

"Did he say where it was located?"

The man removed his hat to scratch a balding head. "No, sir, I don't believe he did. Why?"

"Just wondered—thanks," Jack replied, riding away.

* * *

Smoke was curling from the chimney of the former slave house when Jack pulled Prince to a stop at the gate. The door opened as he dismounted, and his friend Samuel came out. He watched silently as Jack led Prince into the yard. Pausing at the bottom of the steps, Jack motioned toward the horse.

"Samuel, is there somewhere around back where I can put Prince out of sight? I'd just as soon certain people didn't know I was here. We need to talk."

The black face remained stoic and guarded as he gave thought to Jack's request. Finally he spewed a stream of tobacco juice into the sand and motioned with his head for Jack to follow him. Around the house there was a makeshift barn that provided enough shelter for the big thoroughbred. Samuel led Jack inside the meagerly furnished shanty with its scrubbed wood floors. The smell of coffee brewing mingled with the smell of dried grasses used to make rice baskets. It reminded Jack he had not eaten since the night before. Samuel's wife was working over the woodstove, and his longing glance did not go unnoticed by the black man.

"You hungry?"

"Haven't eaten since yesterday."

"Hettie, fix up 'nother plate," Samuel told his wife. "Now, what'd you wanna talk 'bout?"

"I must find Jess. I need his help."

"What you needin' poor Jess fer? Ain't that boy seen his share of trouble?" Samuel asked in a deep voice.

"I'm not here to cause anyone any trouble. Something's going on here, and a lot of good people are getting hurt. Someone needs to get to the bottom of it. All this mystery about Clemdenin Hall, people's crops getting destroyed, and Blacks disappearing . . . I know you can't fight back, but I'm willing to do what I can to help. I may get killed for the trying, but I need your backing and your trust. I don't know who I'm up against or who I can trust."

When Jack finished, Samuel sat in deep thought. His wife's call to breakfast went unheeded. Getting to his feet, he gave Jack a long, searching look. Jack returned his gaze with honesty and restraint.

"What's in it fer you, Cap'n? How do we know you won't be linin' yer own pockets?"

Jack hesitated. He had never been one to talk about himself. "Samuel, there are things you should know."

"We all know who you is, Cap'n. Jess told us about his pappy knowing you. We jest wanna know why you is so anxious t' help us."

"Samuel, my father was a just man. And though I didn't go along with all his cramming religion down my throat, I have lived by the principles he taught me. He owned a large farm in Georgia and raised cotton, but we didn't have slaves. He went through the motions of buying workers at the slave market, but he brought them home and set them free. Many would stay and work for him, and he paid them a wage. It was a well-kept secret.

"My father thought I would follow in his footsteps, but I was a rebellious cuss, and when the war came I joined up to fight. It broke my father's heart, and when the farm was burned to the ground by Sherman's march to the sea, it was more than he could stand. His death, along with the untimely death of my younger brother during the war, took its toll on my mother, and she died of a broken heart. I have seen the best and worst of men. When one man betrays another, I don't cotton to it. During the war I was a victim of one man's betrayal. He is in this area, and I'm here to settle the score. All this other may or may not be related, but I intend to find out. I can't do it without your help."

Samuel had listened without emotion and was about to speak when Hattie came to the door. "Sam'el, is you gonna come 'n' eat these vittles, or do I throw 'em t' them hungry chickens outten there?"

Seated around the small table with its steaming cups of coffee, Samuel bowed his head, and Jack respectfully followed suit as the table prayer was given. Hot plates of eggs, grits, and biscuits were set in front of them. Both men spoke little during the meal. When they had finished, Samuel pushed his plate away to drag his cup toward him, finishing it off. His chair grated noisily on the wooden floor as he slid it back and got to his feet. Jack paused, a biscuit halfway to his mouth.

"Eat—I'll fetch Jess here; you wait," Samuel said and left through the back door.

Jack watched as Hattie scraped the plates and put them to soak in a large metal pan. Then she left him sitting there alone while she went out to throw feed to the chickens, which came running from all directions.

When Jack heard the heavy tread of footsteps on the porch, he realized he had been dozing. How long he had been waiting he could not tell. Samuel came in with Jess and another man, whom he had never seen. They all stood looking at Jack without saying a word. It was Jess who spoke first.

"Sam'el says ya wanna see me?"

"I've been worried about you, Jess. When you didn't come to meet me, I thought something had happened to you. Where've you been?"

"Hidin' out," Jess answered shortly, shifting his weight to the other foot.

"What for?" Jack prodded. "I told you I'd help you."

The three of them exchanged glances before Jess offered an answer. "I didn't like de comp'ny you wuz keepin'."

Jack studied the three stoic faces before him. It suddenly dawned on Jack that he was at their mercy sitting there at the table.

"Aw, Jess—now what do you mean by that?" he said, feigning disgust as he got to his feet to position himself against the door casing. "Didn't you tell him, Samuel?" he asked without taking his eyes off Jess.

"He told me," Jess said and then spat at him. "How d' we know ya ain't tryin' somethin'?"

"Jess, didn't I save your life and help you get away from those men who were wanting to kill you? I made arrangements for Samuel to feed you. What more do you want me to do to prove I'm trying to be your friend?"

"You kin stay away from Clemson!" was Jess's harsh answer.

At the mention of Clemson's name Jack stiffened, and his blood ran cold.

"What did you say?"

"Dat Clemson fella—he's behind all dis!"

Jack looked from one set of accusing eyes to the other, trying to grasp their meaning. How did they know he was on Clemson's trail? He had told Samuel about being betrayed, but he had not mentioned Clemson's name out loud to anyone but Searles, not even to Dreyton. Had someone overheard him talking?

"Clemson is my mortal enemy! I came to make him pay," Jack declared with passion, wondering how these people knew these things. "He betrayed me, and while I rotted in prison my mother died a broken woman!"

"Aw, so dat's it!" Jess breathed, relaxing a little.

"If he's behind all this, you have nothing to fear from me. I'll play it straight. But I need you to help me—"

"Sam'el 'n' Willie here have fam'ly," Jess said, "but I don't have nuttin' t' lose. M' fam'ly's gone except a sister Clemson took. But Sam'el 'n' Willie kin pass de word."

"I need to find you a horse," Jack said thoughtfully.

"Mighty fine one outten in Sam'el's barn," Jess teased. "I almost had him once."

"Hardly, Jess—Prince doesn't take kindly to strangers," Jack replied dryly, "but I won't get you a nag. You're going to need a mount that can run. Ravenswood has some decent horses. I'll get you one and be back after dark. Wait here."

Jack stepped to the door and glanced out. No one appeared to be around except Hattie, who was sitting on the porch of a neighboring house talking to someone inside.

"Samuel, thank you for your hospitality, and please tell Hattie I appreciated the good breakfast. Perhaps this coin will show my gratitude." Jack spoke from the doorway, taking money from his pocket.

"Cap'n, I ain't takin' yer money," Samuel declared, shoving his hand away. "Me 'n' Hattie are glad t' have ya anytime."

Touched by Samuel's words, Jack pulled his hat down on his head to cover his face sufficiently. "Jess, meet me at the ferry at dark. I'll have a horse there for you."

With that he was gone, taking long strides to where Prince waited. Swiftly he mounted and sent the mighty horse into a run, leaping the front fence effortlessly. Three black frames pressed at the front door to watch in awe.

"Well, I do know, Willie—ain't that somethin'?" Samuel grunted.

"Sure is, and that cap'n's somethin' too! Reckon he's shootin' straight with us?" Willie spoke up for the first time.

"Don't be a worryin' none, Willie," Jess responded with a knowing grin, pulling his coat back to expose a large knife sticking in his belt. "He'll play it straight or else."

"Now, Jess, you'd best not be hot-heided. You'll bring down trouble on all us," Samuel warned. "Give the cap'n a chance."

"That I'll be a doin', Sam'el. I'll jest bide my time 'n' keep my head."

* * *

Jack was bone tired and saddle weary when he rode Prince around to the stable at Ravenswood's place. He was turning the reins over to the stable boy when he was hailed by a friendly voice from the house.

"Jack! Back so soon?"

"Hello, Sandy! Had to run an errand down this way. Hope you don't mind."

"Not at all. Come in. Glad to have the company."

"Before I do, have you got a horse I can buy? I promised a friend I'd pick him up a good horse."

Jack waited until Ravenswood thumped his way down the steps to where he stood. For a man with only one leg, he was certainly agile.

"Well, sir, let's see," Ravenswood muttered, scrubbing the short stubble of beard on his chin. "I've got a spirited roan out there, but it'd take a real man to ride him. Who ya buyin' it fer?"

"It's a man. Let's take a look at him. Can he run?"

"I've never ridden him, but the stableboy says he runs like the wind," Ravenswood answered, leading the way into the stall where the roan was. "Wanna try 'im out?"

"No thanks—I've had all the riding I want for one day," Jack answered with a grimace, running an experienced hand over the horse's flank and down his legs. "I'll take your word for it."

"Ya do look plum tuckered out," Ravenswood noted, giving him an appraising glance.

Jack leaned to look at a hoof. "Do you have the saddle and headgear?"

"Sure do. It's a good saddle—broke in real nice."

"What's your price?"

"Lemme see," Ravenswood began, scratching his shaggy head vigorously, "How 'bout 50 dollahs fer it all?"

"Fair enough," Jack agreed, moving out toward the house. "Have him ready by dark. Do you mind if I rest awhile?"

"Well, I'd rather chew the fat with ya, but I can see ya need the rest. Ya know where the room is." Ravenswood laughed, pulling himself up the steps.

"I'm sure beholden to you, Sandy," Jack said with feeling.

"Should I have ya wakened fer supper?" Ravenswood called after him as he headed up the stairs.

"Sure thing."

*   *   *

Only a thin sliver of moon along with a myriad of stars shone down on the dark figure waiting in the shadows of a live oak tree. Night creatures gave off an endless rhythmic song. Somewhere a fish jumped. From where he stood, Jack could see the feeble light of a lantern in the pilot house of the ferry. Hearing the slight scrape of a boot behind him, he turned to see a shadow moving toward him. It was Jess.

"Cap'n?" came the hoarse whisper.

"Right here, Jess," Jack responded, handing Jess the reins of the roan. "The ferry is empty. If you're ready, we'll cross now. Don't talk—just listen. Keep your head turned away. Let's go."

The two made their way to the ferry and boarded. In a matter of moments they were headed for the opposite shore. The man handling the night shift was less talkative than the earlier ferry worker. All efforts Jack made for conversation were answered with grunts, as the man peered through the darkness to where Jess was standing.

"Kinda unusual t' see a Black out this time o' night," he muttered to Jack, who declined to answer. Jack kept his distance from Jess. It was just as well they not be tied together.

Once on the other side, Jack mounted Prince and rode off up the road where he paused to wait for Jess, who took his time in getting there. The ferry was already on its return to the opposite shore.

Impatient to be on his way, Jack was just about to go back to see what had happened to Jess when he heard him coming.

"Cap'n, dis is sure some hoss ya picked out fer me. When I climbed into dat saddle, he jest hunched up and near tossed me in de river. Taken me awhile t' show him who's boss."

Jack felt laughter well up inside him and was glad the darkness hid his face. Turning Prince, he headed away, unable to speak for fear of betraying himself.

"Ravenswood said he was a spirited horse and it would take a real man to handle him," Jack offered when he could trust his voice. "I guess you're that man, Jess. Let's ride."

Dawn found the two weary travelers just outside the town of Charleston. The ferry was waiting to cross Ashley River. Jack pulled Prince to a stop a short distance away.

"Jess, here's some money. Find a place to stay. Try to get on down to the city market. If you can, go there each day to mingle, and keep your ears open. I'll keep in touch with you there or leave messages with the basket weaver who sits in the center east end of the building off Meeting Street. She knows me. I did her a favor once."

Jess accepted the money with a nod and rode the roan down onto the waiting boat. Jack waited for a few minutes and followed suit. Neither spoke or acknowledged one another's presence. Jack chatted for a few minutes with the pilot, but when the fellow began to ask questions, he moved off. The less people knew about him the better.

On the other side Jess rode on, and Jack turned to the right to head for his room and a clean bed, which sounded awfully good to him at the moment. Tonight he was to meet with Tom Searles again. Since he had learned little to tell him, he was at a loss. Until he knew more, perhaps he could get by with alluding to some things he had heard. He'd have to think on it.

Jess rode on to where unpaved streets muffled the sound of the roan's hoofs. The closely built houses all looked the same. At the end of a street, he reined in before a house not too different from the one he grew up in. He slid from the saddle. Somewhere a baby's cry mingled with the bark of a dog.

Opening the makeshift gate, he led the horse inside the yard and looped the reins to a post holding the roof of the porch. A dim light was showing through the crack under the door as he mounted the steps. He heard the scrape of a chair, then cautious footsteps in answer to his knock.

"Who out dere?" a deep voice inquired.

"You be Mose?" Jess answered in a low voice.

"I be. Who be wantin' t' know?"

"Name's Jess. Sam'el down on de Edisto sent me."

The door opened a crack, and Jess stood quietly as dark, suspicious eyes looked him over, taking in the roan tied to the porch. Satisfied there was no threat, the man swung the door wide, allowing Jess to enter, closing it behind him before speaking.

"What yo' be wantin'?"

"Kin we talk?" Jess asked, his eyes sweeping over three youngsters asleep on a pallet on the floor.

He was led into the kitchen, and a door between the two rooms was pushed shut. In the better light, Jess could see Mose was probably in his early 50s. His angular face and light color spoke of the mixing of the races, not unusual in the day of slavery. Black hair graying a little at the temples lent a sense of dignity to the serene face.

"I take it Sam'el's all right, since he sent yo'."

"Yes suh, he be jest fine. Say t' give ya his regards." Jess grinned.

"Now, whatcha wanna talk about?" Mose asked, pulling out a chair at the table and motioning for Jess to sit. Taking another chair, he waited for Jess to speak.

Jess related the incidents of the previous days leading up to Captain Brevard's coming to them for help. He was just finishing his story when a woman came stomping the sand from her feet at the back door.

"Whatcha wantin' from me?" Mose asked Jess tersely.

"Somewhere t' stay. I'll pay. Don' want t' be no burden."

"Pay I's not a worryin' 'bout—trouble I is," Mose said with emotion. "I's got a fam'ly!"

"Don't ya think I ain't seen dat?" Jess replied heatedly. "Jist help me find a bed where I kin hide out. I'll come 'n' go real careful."

"I'll think on it," Mose returned with a frown, glancing up at his wife with worried eyes as she poured them some coffee. "Man's gotta be lookin' at what he's gettin' hisself into."

Jess remained quiet, watching Mose's wife place a pan of bread into the oven. The room had grown quite warm, and Mose reached to push the back door open wider.

"Loose dat door 'hind yo', Jess. Let some of dis heat in t' de youngins."

Jess complied, knowing there was no more use in pressing his case. The answer would come in due time. Instead, he asked questions about the town of Charleston, finding Mose was a good source of information.

"It ain't good for no black man t' be in some places, unless dey's workin' fer de white folks—dat's mos'ly down by de water, 'n' de batt'ry," Mose warned, pulling his chair forward as his wife placed a plate of biscuits in front of them, along with fried side meat. "Help yo'self t' some of dat meat dere."

When they were finished eating, Mose led Jess to the outside. "See dat barn over dere?" he said, pointing off in the distance. "Dat belongs t' Crawfish Brown, 'n' it's gotta loft. Say I sent yo'. Dere'll be food brung yo'. Fetch yo' horse 'n' go out de back."

With a wave of his hand to Mose, Jess led the roan off across the field in the morning sunlight. Crawfish was out feeding his stock and straightened up to watch Jess coming toward him.

"Mornin'," Jess sang out.

"Mawnin' yersef," Crawfish returned, folding his arms on the top of the fence, bucket still in hand. He was a big man, and dark muscles exposed to the golden glow of the sun rippled and glistened. A wide grin spread across his face, exposing a row of white teeth.

"Mose wants ya to know he sent me. I need some place t' hide. He says ya have a loft in yer barn."

"There's a gate 'round on the other side—yer welcome," Crawfish indicated, motioning with his head. "Put yer hoss in that first stall. I'll be done here in a minute."

Jess did as he was told, removing the saddle and halter. Crawfish came in with a bucket of feed for the roan. "Ya don' have no bedroll?" he asked, taking note Jess had nothing with him.

"Don't have no time t' collect things when yer runnin'," Jess replied.

"Don't reckon a fella would," Crawfish agreed, laying a big hand on his shoulder. "I'll get a blanket. Hay's up there; scatter some out."

"I's gonna be goin' in 'n' out. Won't bother ya none."

"It's ya'll's life—do with it whatcha want," Crawfish shrugged, leaving him.

Jess wearily climbed the homemade ladder and spread the hay for a bed. Stretching out, he slept almost immediately. Even the gentle touch of a dark hand on his failed to wake him.

*I*T WAS LATE IN THE DAY when Jack opened his eyes. He had been asleep for hours. He struggled groggily to a sitting position. A glance out the window told him the day was well spent. Rubbing his beard, he decided he would never wear another one after this episode was over. It gave him the feeling of never having a clean face.

Pushing off the bed, he stepped into his trousers and moved to wash his face. The dark shirt he took from his saddlebag was fraying around the collar. All the better for his disguise, Jack thought, as he surveyed his rather careless, well-worn attire. Fastening his gun belt low around his waist, he donned the dusty, black broad-brimmed plantation hat he had been wearing, pulling it low over his eyes.

Something to eat was very much on his mind when he stepped into the empty hall and made his way down the front stairs to the lobby. As was his habit, Jack paused in the doorway, taking note of the activity in the street, then stepped out. Across the street and up the way a little was a small eating place he had frequented before when in Charleston. The food was good there, so he made his way toward it.

As he neared his destination, suddenly Cordelia Dureen appeared, escorted closely by Wilford Crenshaw. They emerged from the building and made their way toward him. She glanced up at him, and the look of gladness in her eyes turned to one of puzzled dismay as Jack turned abruptly to look in a store window, waiting for them to pass.

"What is it, my dear?" Crenshaw asked anxiously, noting her expression.

"Nothing, Wilford—that man reminded me of a good friend I know," she said loudly enough for Jack to hear.

In the glass he could see Wilford Crenshaw cast a curious glance in his direction without recognition, but he was sure Cordelia knew who he was, for she flashed a smile at his reflection.

When they had passed on to a waiting buggy, Jack sauntered casually on into the diner. Of all the people in Charleston, Cordelia Dureen was the last one he wished to run into. It seemed she was everywhere.

Seeing her together with Wilford Crenshaw did not improve his mood. He ate the food placed before him, somberly listening with little interest to the conversation of a couple of men at a table nearby. They appeared to be planters, for their talk centered around crops.

It wasn't until he heard the mention of Clemson's name that he glanced over at them. One was a short, swarthy individual who spoke with an accent. The other, a taller man with graying hair and piercing, hawklike eyes, caught his undivided attention. It was he who had spoken of Clemson.

"He's wantin' t' buy my land," he went on heatedly. "My back's t' the wall, 'n' I don't know what t' do. Can't get any more money from Crenshaw. It's gonna be hard on the wife if we have t' pull stakes again. 'N' I'm about t' the place where I'm ready t' take matters int' my own hands, if ya know what I mean."

The swarthy character gave a knowing look at his companion, who patted the gun he wore. "Nothin' ain't ever gained by killin', Medford," he said with little humor, "'ceptin' a hangin'. That'd be harder on the missus than findin' a new place. 'Sides, you ain't never shot that thing since the war. You probably couldn't hit the broad side of a barn."

"Guess you're right," Medford replied with resignation. "The war took all that kind of fightin' outta me." He slammed his fist down hard on the table, making the dishes jump. "Why can't that man offer me more money? My place's worth twice what he's offerin'."

"Don't take on so, George—you'll work yourself into a stroke or somethin'."

"I'm sorry, Joseph," Medford replied, his shoulders sagging with the futility of it all. "It just eats at my gut t' be over a barrel like this. I was countin' on that crop t' pull us out."

A chair scraped, and the short, swarthy man called Joseph stood up. "I gotta go, George. Keep in touch. I wish I could loan you the money, but you know how it is with me."

Medford sat staring glumly at the wall after his companion walked out. Jack pushed back his plate and took a small piece of paper from his pocket. He scribbled a note on it and took it to the girl at the counter.

"After I've gone," he instructed, handing her the money for his supper along with the piece of paper, "give this note to that man sitting over there." He pointed to Medford.

Once outside, he headed back to his room to wait. If Medford responded to the note, he should arrive soon.

"If a man comes in asking for John Blosser, send him up," he instructed the man behind the desk.

"Yes sir, Mr. Blosser."

Medford stared in disbelief at the note handed to him.

> I can help you.
> Come to the inn
> across the street
> and ask for John
> Blosser.

"Who gave this t' ya?" he asked.

"The man who was sitting at that table," she responded, pointing to where Jack had been.

Medford remembered vaguely there was someone there but had been so engrossed in his own troubles he had paid little attention to those around him. He dropped a coin on the table and went out. Glancing both ways, he walked up toward the inn. He paused, as if trying to decide on a course of action. Making sure no one saw him enter, he stepped into the lobby and went to the desk.

"Is there a Mr. Blosser here?" he asked.

"Last door on the left before you hit the back stairs," the clerk answered without looking up.

Jack heard the heavy tread on the stairs and moved his chair away from the window. He would need to get this over with quickly, for the slanting rays of the sun told him the time was swiftly coming for his meeting with Searles.

Footsteps sounded outside the door, and there was a pause before the knock. Medford was a cautious man. That was good. Counting on the man's desperation, Jack waited until the second timid rap before going to open the door.

"Did ya wish t' see me?" Medford asked in a low voice, glancing both ways in the darkened hall.

Jack stepped back to allow him to enter. Medford licked his lips nervously as his eyes took in the room at a glance, coming at last to the big gun hanging at Jack's hip. Waiting until the man's eyes returned to his, Jack smiled.

"Mr. Medford, I couldn't help overhearing your plight. I didn't mean to listen in on your conversation, but it was unavoidable with the tables so close. I want to help you—and myself.

"Here's my proposition. I will enter into a partnership with you and provide money for a new crop. You stay on the land and work it. We'll split the proceeds of the crop 50/50. When I receive my investment back plus interest, the land is yours."

A look of disbelief spread across Medford's face as the words penetrated his troubled mind. Walking over to the chair, he dropped as one whose legs could no longer hold him up.

"Ya don't even know me," Medford said shakily.

"I know about you through a mutual friend," Jack replied, "and I'm a fair judge of character. Is it a deal?"

"Mister, I'm a God-fearin' man, 'n' I keep my word—yes, it's a deal," Medford exclaimed, holding out a trembling hand.

"There is only one requirement," Jack warned, taking his hand. "This must remain a secret between you and me. No one— I repeat, *no one*, not even your wife—is to know. Just tell them you were able to borrow the money from an investor in Atlanta. Agreed?"

"Agreed," Medford answered, getting to his feet and squaring his shoulders. "I can be as closed-mouth as the next un, Mr. Blosser."

"The name is Captain Andrew Jackson Brevard to you. John Blosser is an alias I use."

"Aw, now," Medford breathed, "I've heard of ya. Folks lived down near Atlanta. Fine man, your father. You were one of Colonel Stothard's men."

"I was. But you must never mention my name to anyone. I am here to settle an old score. If something happens to me, your debt will be clear."

"Clemson?"

"Yes. Where is he?"

"Don't rightly know. I've heard people mention Clemdenin Hall, but nobody seems t' know anythin' 'bout it."

"What's he look like now?" Jack pressed.

"Can't say. Ain't seen him 'ceptin' at night. Big man. Sits his horse kinda hunkered over. Don't talk much."

"Keep your ears open, and find out more for me if you can," Jack instructed, walking to the door. "Meanwhile, I'll have some papers drawn up and write a draft for what you owe at the bank. There's a little café on East Bay. Meet me there in two days to sign them." He opened the door to look into the hall. "Might be a good idea to stay in town. It'd be safer. Man could get killed riding in the dark alone. The coast is clear—good night."

Medford wanted to ride out to share the news with his wife, but Jack's warning held him in check. It was best not to do anything foolish, he decided, and stopped at the desk to pay for a room. Neither he nor the clerk detected the quiet footsteps on the back stairs.

By the time Jack had Prince saddled, it had grown quite dark. Searles would be expecting him. He led Prince out and stepped into the saddle.

Tom Searles was waiting for him in the drawing room when Mantie showed him in. "Thought you wasn't gonna show," he growled, taking a long draught on his cigar.

"Got held up right at the last moment," Jack explained.

"What'd you find out?"

"Been working on setting a plan in motion," Jack said. "It's going to take time. A man needs to be seen in a certain pattern to set up an alibi. You want this done nice and clean, don't you?"

"Sure, take yer time—things just seem longer when you've got nothin' t' do but sit 'n' think, I guess," Searles mumbled, sighing loudly.

"How's your legs today?"

"Been hurtin' somethin' awful," Tom answered, shifting the cover over his legs. "Must be a storm comin'."

"Well, it's been a busy day, Tom. I hope you don't mind if I don't stay long. I'm careful about activities these days."

Rising from his chair, Jack reached for his hat. "Guess I'll mosey along, Tom, and get some shut-eye."

"Where you stayin', Jack?" Searles asked, taking the cigar from his mouth to brush the ashes off onto the floor.

"At the Charlestonian. You know, that little inn across—"

"Yeah, I know where it is," Searles broke in.

"If you need me, send a message to the desk," Jack said from the door. "If I'm not out tracking, I'll come running."

"All right. Keep in touch. If you see Mantie, send her in here. Good night."

Pausing in the hall to put his hat on, Jack noticed a pair of boots sitting next to a hall tree. Black muck was caked around the soles. A closer look and the swipe of his forefinger let him know the boots had been worn that very day. Knowing Searles would be listening for the door to close, he hurried out. He had left Prince by the back gate, so he headed that way.

An idea hit him as he passed the stable. The door gave way easily, and he slipped silently in. Feeling his way in the dark, he found Searles's big horse right away. "Steady, boy," Jack whispered, running his hand down the legs to the fetlocks. A dry substance was clinging to the hairs. Pulling a piece loose, he found it bore the odor of muck found in the lowlands. He slipped out and found his way to where Prince waited.

Mounting up, he stared at the dim light showing through the window. It was obvious Searles was lying about his legs. But why? Suddenly it dawned on him something was terribly wrong, and he wondered what other secrets this house held.

Riding along the dark street, Jack reflected on his conversations with Searles. Could it be Tom Searles was lying to him about many things? Thinking back on it, he was relieved he had not told Searles of his recent activities.

"Prince, looks like you and me are treading on thin ice; there's more to this than appears to be," he muttered, taking note of the shadowy hiding places around him. "A man could get shot around here mighty easy."

Jack urged Prince into a fast trot and was relieved when he reached the safety of his room. Jack removed his shoes, blew out the lamp, and stretched out on the bed to think. He had been in the area for several days and had not laid eyes on Clemson. In fact, the only mention of his name had been by Jack himself, Searles, Medford, and Jess, who had accused him of being in with Clemson. Jess had said Clemson was a big man. So had Medford. As near as he could remember, Clemson had been of slender stature and less than six feet tall. Passing years had a way of changing a person's appearance, though.

Racking his brain for all the pieces, Jack still could not make them fit together. Tomorrow he would seek out Jess.

With this settled in his mind, he turned his thoughts to Cordelia Dureen. She had recognized him, yet she had not given him away to Crenshaw. What an intriguing woman! He felt his pulses quicken at the memory of the smile she had sent his way.

As slumber overtook him, a sweet face with flashing dark eyes continued to haunt him.

*   *   *

Outside her home, Cordelia thanked her escort and mounted the stairs to her room. Why she had accepted Wilford Crenshaw's invitation for dinner and a concert she did not know, for she found his persistent proposals of marriage tiring. While all her friends thought Crenshaw a great catch, she shuddered at having to spend the rest of her life with him.

Captain Jack Brevard came to mind as she sat down before the mirror to remove the pins from coils of black hair piled high on her head, letting it cascade around her shoulders. In fact, she had thought a lot about him lately, wondering if he was still in Charleston. Though happy to see him there on the street, she was puzzled at his behavior. Was it because she was with Crenshaw? She doubted that. There must be another reason. John Dreyton had alluded to the fact he was in the area on a private mission. Was it because he was in danger? The thought startled her, bringing something akin to fear for his safety. Did his presence here have anything to do with what was going on in the lowlands?

Although her brother refused to discuss his problems, Cordelia had overheard conversations among the men who had come to their home. Even the Blacks working for him lived in fear, whispering among themselves about nightriders preying on the people.

"Well, Captain, perhaps you and I should have a nice long chat," she said to her image in the mirror.

She would find out where he was staying and send a message. Satisfied with this decision, she slipped into her gown and sought her bed. Sleep did not come soon, however, for she kept going over in her mind what she would say to him when they met. But inevitably her thoughts kept going back to that night on the veranda at Dreyton Hall when he had bared his soul to her. Had it humiliated him so much he did not wish to see her again?

Little did he know how it had affected her. Dealing with her own emotions had not been easy. Overcome, she had fought the desire to lay her head against his shoulder—to tell him it was all right, that she understood. Had he not taken her in when he did, she would have betrayed herself. The heat came into her face as she recalled that moment.

Cordelia lay thinking of all she knew about this fascinating man. He had come from a good family, a Christian family. He was neat in appearance, even in his traveling clothes. He did not drink or smoke, and he knew how to treat a lady. Unlike many of the men she had known, he had not been bold, nor did he seek to make unwanted advances toward her.

He was respected by men like Sanford Ravenswood and John Dreyton, and though Dreyton had been hesitant to talk about Jack, Cordelia knew Ravenswood would tell her what she wanted to know. Mentally she vowed to join Tammy Sue again for a visit there in the near future.

How long she lay thinking about Jack Brevard Cordelia did not know, but before falling asleep she came to grips with her feelings. Before she had met the captain she had been happy with her life. Though she had not taken her suitors seriously, she had enjoyed their company. Restless and preoccupied of late, she had grown weary of their overtures. It was only at her brother's urging that she had accepted Crenshaw's persistent invitation to dinner. Once again it had proved to be dull and boring.

Seeing Jack Brevard there on the street this evening had quickened the beat of her heart and left her breathless. It was then that Cordelia realized she was more than just fascinated with the handsome Captain Brevard.

7

A LIGHT TOUCH ON HIS HAND startled Jess awake. When he opened his eyes, a handsome young black woman gasped and quickly withdrew her hand.

"I thought you wuz dead!" she exclaimed, her eyes growing wide. "You ain't moved or even used the blanket I brung you last night."

"A man what's ridden all night is gonna be tired, woman, 'n' be needin' his sleep. He don't be needin' the likes of you pokin' 'round him t' see iffen he's dead," Jess answered, lifting his head to take in the blanket at his feet.

"Well, I guess ya won't be a wantin' these biscuits and side meat I brung ya, huh?" she replied saucily, removing the flour sack bag she had laid on the straw.

"Don't ya be takin' m' bread, woman—jest 'cause a man be tired don't mean he ain't hungry," Jess warned, raising up unexpectedly to grab her arm. Propping himself against some hay, he proceeded to devour the contents of the bag.

"Wha's yer name?" he mumbled with a mouth full of biscuit.

"Cally."

"How old be ya?"

"Old enough," Cally answered, raising her chin.

"Fer what?"

"Fer marryin'!"

"Uh huh. Fer marryin' who?"

"Ain't seen nobody I'd have yet."

"Dat so?" Jess said, finishing off the last of the food. "If ya be thinkin' I'm gonna be axin', yer wrong. I's a busy man, in dangerous work."

"I knows all that," she retorted, retreating down the ladder to call up to him, "an' I wouldn't be marryin' with the likes of you, nohow."

Jess rolled his head back in laughter as she fled from the barn. He crawled over to the small window overlooking the barnyard to watch her storm into the house.

"Now ain't she somethin'? She sho' is!"

Glancing up at the sun, Jess realized it was time he should be moseying to the market. From the loft he could see the countryside pretty well. Off in the distance a wide river lay shimmering in the morning light. From the direction he was facing he knew it must be the Cooper.

Jess hoisted himself over the side of the loft to find the first rung of the ladder. Down below he met Crawfish coming into the barn.

"Mawnin'!"

"Mawnin' yersef, Crawfish," Jess returned. "Be dere water someplace where a man kin wash the sleep from his eye?"

"There be a pump at the waterin' trough back of the barn. Help yersef."

Jess headed in that direction. He was splashing away when Crawfish came out to stand and watch him for a minute.

"No soap?" he asked.

"Nope."

"Ah'll have Cally fetch ya some."

"Is she yer daughter?" Jess asked, shaking the water from his hands.

"She's my granddaughter. Mighty fine gal, too, so don't ya be takin' on with her, or you'll be reckonin' with me. Understand?"

"Sho' do, Crawfish. Sho' do. Now iffen you'll tell me de hurryinest way t' market, I'll be a-goin'."

It was farther to the main part of town than he had imagined, but he enjoyed the walk. The market was teeming with activity when he arrived, and he blended into the crowd. Every section of market space was taken up by wagons loaded with vegetables, crates of squawking chickens, homemade bread, cheese, rice, indigo, and baskets.

Jess wandered through the building looking for the basket weaver where he was to meet Jack. She sat on a short stool that barely supported her ponderous weight, hands busy with the basket she was working on. He caught her curious glance when she looked up to find him watching her.

"Would there be somethin' yer wantin', Mista?" she asked, reaching for another piece of grass on the ground by her.

Jess moved nearer to her side. Picking up a basket, he held it up to look at it.

"Cap'n Brevard told me t' meet him here; said it'd be toler'ble with ya," he said softly, his eyes shifting to her round countenance. The woman's expression changed, and she shifted her weight on the stool, stretching a foot out before her.

"Yes suh, sho' is gonna be a hot one!" she answered loudly enough for others nearby to hear. "Well, don't be standin' there doin' nothin'. Start strippin' grass. I'm sho' 'nuff gonna need a heap more 'fo' this basket be done."

Startled, Jess dropped the basket and jumped to do her bidding. There had been something of a warning in her voice. He glanced out of the corner of his eye to see a man in a dark blue shirt and black pants tucked into high-topped boots staring at them from the doorway of an adjoining building. The high-crowned black hat he wore hid his eyes, but Jess noticed he wore a full mustache.

"Wait'll I tell yer pa all ya was a wantin' t' do was play with the baskets 'n' dream," she went on in a scolding voice, her fingers expertly working the grass in and out to form a pattern. "He'll be fer keepin' ya home t' chop cotton."

Jess did not reply but kept his head low as he worked. He did not look up again until he heard the woman's whisper.

"He's gone!"

"Who wuz he?"

"Nightrider," she whispered, leaning close.

The very word struck terror to Jess's heart. Had he been recognized? The woman must have sensed the agitation, for she laid a comforting hand on his shoulder.

"Jist hold steady. Don't ya be lettin' 'em think ya got somethin' t' be scared of. Keep yer eyes seein' 'n' ears lis'nin'."

She was right, of course. To be a help to the captain, he'd have to find the courage to outsmart his enemies.

"What's yer name?" she asked in a whisper. Out loud she said, "Han' me some mo' o' dat grass."

"Jess," he whispered back, handing her a handful of grass strips.

"I'll call ya Jamie. My sister's boy. Call me Auntie."

Jess nodded his acknowledgment and went on with his work. One other time he looked up to see the man studying them. This time instead of turning away, the man strolled over to where they were. Up close he appeared taller.

"I see ya got some new hep today, Mary. Kin of yers?"

"Yes suh," the black woman answered coolly. "He's m' sister's boy from up Goose Creek way. Come down t' hep me while the mista is stove up."

"What's yo' name, boy?"

When Jess hesitated, the man poked him with his boot. "Speak up, boy!"

"Jamie, suh," Jess replied, pitching his voice higher than normal. "I's m' mammy's firstborn, suh."

"I could swear I've seen ya before," the man said, stroking the beard on his chin.

"Ya ever been up here b'fo', Jamie?" Mary asked casually.

"No, ma'am—'ceptin' when I's a youngun," Jess replied in the same high-pitched voice.

"Hmph." The large man didn't look convinced but turned to leave.

As a sign of defiance, Mary spit in the dust where he had stood.

"He'll be back?" Jess asked.

"He'll be back—they don't give up," she replied, getting to her feet. "Watch my baskets. You'll be safe fer a spell."

Jess watched her disappear in the crowd, then leaned back against the building to observe people moving to and fro among the wagons. A well-dressed woman with red hair moved into view, carrying a parasol. Beside her was a young black girl, dressed lavishly, arms filled with purchases. Jess had never seen anything like her, and she captured his attention. So intent was he in his admiration that he fairly jumped at the sound of a voice nearby.

"Go slow, Jess—she's not for you," Jack cautioned.

"I's Jamie," Jess said, demonstrating his new voice to the captain. "I's the basket lady's nephew."

Jack smiled and nodded. "Good thinking. Where's Mary?"

"I dunno. She told me t' watch 'er baskets, den jest up 'n' left. Dere's been a man watchin' me. Came over actin' kinda mean, wantin' t' know my name. But Auntie stuck up fer me. Tole 'im I's her sister's boy from up 'round Goose Creek way. After he wuz gone, she says he's a nightrider."

Jack knelt down and picked up one of the baskets. "What did he look like?"

"Near tall as you, only more meat on 'is bones. Blue shirt, 'n' black britches tucked in t' dem tall-like boots. His eyes sent shivers down m' back. He had a mustache too. It kinda hung aroun' 'is mouth."

Jack's mind went back to that dark night at the cabin. Could this be the same man who did the speaking for the group that awful night? From what he could see in the light of the torches, the spokesman had a mustache. If so, was he working for someone here in Charleston? Clemson, maybe?

"Where are you staying?"

"Out at Crawfish's barn," Jess answered softly, after looking around.

"How can I find you?"

"Jist go out Meetin' Street almost t' the end 'n' look t' yer left one street over. Dat's it."

"Did ya wanna buy a basket, Mista?" It was Mary's voice. "Don't look 'roun', Cap'n," she went on in a whisper. "That man is back agin, 'n' he jest keeps on a lookin'."

Jack lifted a basket, turning it around in his hand. Pulling out some coins, he offered one to Mary.

"Thank ya, suh," Mary exclaimed, a broad smile spreading across her ebony face. "Good day to ya!"

Jack moved away into the building before the man, where he could observe him without being seen. There seemed to be something familiar about the set of the shoulders and the way he held his head. If he could only hear him speak, he would know for sure. Little chance for that, for the man had swung away into the crowd.

Jack followed him, shopping along as he went. At the end of the long building, the man mounted up and rode off south on Bay toward the Battery. It was then Jack knew for sure. The rider at the cabin that dreadful night and this man were one and the same. He stood watching until the rider turned west, toward Searles's place.

"Now why do you suppose he's riding out that way?" he murmured softly to himself. Retracing his steps to where Mary and Jess were, Jack knelt on one knee beside her. "Mary, do you know who that man is?"

"I axed around, 'n' they who know say he go by name of Baxter Spriggs. Ever'body say he's a mean one."

"Did they say where he lives?"

"No, suh—they jest seen him down around the battery, lots of times."

"Has he ever been seen near Searles's place?"

"Yes, Cap'n. Som've wondered iffen he live over in there. Why you axin' me all these questions?" She turned puzzled eyes on him.

"It is safer for you not to know, Mary," Jack responded with compassion, laying a hand on her shoulder. "Let's just say.

I'm trying to help Jess and your friends. Jess, I'll look you up tonight."

Jack left them and headed for the inn where he was staying. Entering the lobby, he was hailed by the desk clerk. "There's a message for you, sir."

"Thank you."

Jack waited until he was in his room to open the note addressed to Captain Jack Brevard in neat, dainty handwriting.

Dear Captain Brevard:

I need to talk with you. Would you come to supper? I am staying at my home on South Battery. The name is beside the door. I'll expect you at seven.

Cordelia Dureen

Clutching the paper in his hand, Jack sank onto the bed in disbelief. After the way he had acted that night at Dreyton Hall, he had not expected her ever to want to see him again. She had said she needed to talk to him. Was she in trouble?

He looked down at the clothes he was wearing. They would have to do. Going to the mirror, Jack surveyed his bearded image, longing for the day when he could shave. Right now he could not risk being recognized. At least a trim might be in order.

He returned to the lobby. It was empty except for a man asleep in a chair, hat down over his face. Jack learned from the clerk that there was a barber on the next street. On the way he passed a haberdashery and turned back to purchase a new shirt.

When asked if there was a livery stable where he might get a horse, the barber informed him of one. He had already decided not to ride Prince. With Baxter Spriggs and his men in the area, they would be quick to recognize the big chestnut stallion. The sorrel horse he chose was a sturdy, intelligent animal with a good gait—not like Prince, but he would do.

The day was well spent when Jack finally headed back to his room. On the way he made another decision. Come morning, he would move to a different location. Leaving the sorrel at the hitching post outside the stable, he mounted the stairs two at a time to enter the darkening rear hallway. The sound of hurried footsteps and the shadow of a man making for the front stairs aroused his suspicion.

He paused to listen at the door of his room and found it had been left slightly ajar. There was no movement in the room beyond. He had caught whoever it was in the act of leaving.

But still, being a cautious man, he moved to one side, pulling his revolver. He pushed the door wide open and waited. When no response came, he stepped in and closed the door. In disarray on the bed were the contents of his saddlebags. Nothing had been taken. Apparently the motive was not robbery. Empty drawers in the small chest were left open, bearing mute evidence of the haste in which the man had been searching for something.

"Probably wanting to find out who I am," Jack muttered to himself, shoving his gun in its holster. It had always been a habit of his to avoid leaving his identity on anything he owned. Once again it had paid off.

Whoever it was probably thought he was looking through the pack of a beggar, Jack through grimly as he stuffed his few belongings back into the saddlebags.

Heading down to the lobby, he glanced at the big clock ticking away on the wall behind the desk. If he hurried, there would be time to seek out another place to stay before keeping his appointment with Cordelia.

"Leavin' town?" the clerk asked, when Jack stepped up to ask for his bill.

"Reckon so," Jack answered curtly, giving the clerk a measured look. Had he provided entrance for the intruder? There had been no signs of a forced entry.

"Where ya headed?" the clerk asked, much too casually.

"Sometimes it's unhealthy to know too much," Jack responded coldly, tossing a coin on the book.

The clerk's face paled, and he stammered an apology, which Jack ignored, taking the lower hall to the stable. In a matter of moments he had Prince saddled. The shorter days worked in his favor as he led Prince out to mount up. Picking up the reins of the sorrel, he made his way through the back streets of the city toward the black sector of town. Turning into Meeting Street, he went on past the railroad shops and turntable until he came to the edge of town. Just as Jess had said, he could see the dim outline of Crawfish's barn off to the left and headed for it.

From his lofty perch, Jess heard the sound of horses below. Holding his breath, he remained very still, peering into the darkness. The horses stopped just outside the gate, and a familiar voice came through the darkness.

"Jess."

"Cap'n, is dat you out dere?"

"Yes. How do I get in?"

"Jist a minute," Jess answered, scrambling down the ladder to appear in the barnyard. "Over dis way, Cap'n."

Jack stepped down and tied the sorrel on the outside, then led Prince through the gate Jess held open.

"I'll get Crawfish," Jess whispered and disappeared.

"Crawfish, dis is my frien' Cap'n Jack," Jess explained when he returned. "He's de man what's been helpin' me."

"Evenin', Cap'n," Crawfish greeted in his low voice.

From what he could see in the dim light, Jack could tell Crawfish was a big man. "Folks, I need help," Jack said. "I need someplace safe to leave Prince and wondered if there might be a stall empty here where Jess could look after him." He told them of the search of his room, finishing with, "If they see Prince, they'll know who I am."

Jess hesitated, waiting for Crawfish to speak.

"It's fine with me, Jess, long as he pays fer the hay."

"I intended to, Crawfish," Jack asserted, reaching in his pocket for some money. "Will this do for now?"

"Sho', Cap'n Jack. Jist bring him on in here. Jess, go ahead of him 'n' strike a match t' that lantern."

Jack saw Prince safely in the stall, then mounted the sorrel. "Jess, I've got to ride. I'll be back later. Sleep light!"

Jack nudged the rented horse off down the dusty road at a fast trot. Cutting across the narrow peninsula, he purposely wound through narrow streets to avoid being observed by Spriggs's men. Just after 7:00, he pulled the sorrel up in front of a stately two-story home on the South Battery.

Securing the reins to the hitching post, he mounted the circular steps and knocked. Cordelia Dureen, dressed in light blue, answered the door.

"Captain Brevard, I was about to give you up!"

"I apologize for being late, Miss Dureen," Jack found himself saying. "I—I was delayed by something unforeseen."

"I'm so glad you came," she assured him, taking his hat. "Come in."

Jack looked around him as she disappeared into another room. He could hear her talking to someone. Comfortably furnished, the room revealed the touch of a woman with good taste. Over the mantel was the portrait of a handsome young man in a Confederate uniform. Jack stared at it. How much it reminded him of the many gallant men who fought and died on both sides of a war that should never have happened!

"He was killed early on in the war," Cordelia spoke behind him. He had not heard her enter the room.

"Your brother?"

"No. John Dureen, my husband. We were married just before he marched off to battle. He never came back."

"You loved him?"

"Very much."

"You have not married. Are you still in love with him?" Jack asked, turning toward her so he could see her eyes.

"His memory will always be dear to me, Captain, but I do not believe in loving ghosts," she responded. "I learned a long time ago the living must go on."

"You are an attractive woman, Miss—Mrs. Dureen, yet you have not married," Jack found himself repeating. It seemed he was standing on the edge of a precipice.

"Perhaps, Captain, I have not found such a man to take his place," she replied, the color heightening in her cheeks. "Come. The table should be ready."

She led him through the formal dining room to a cozy, candlelit alcove just off the kitchen. "I hope you will find this comfortable, Captain. The dining room seems so formal."

Jack helped her with her chair and seated himself. The smell of food reminded him he had not eaten since breakfast. No good at small talk, he ate and listened politely while she talked, watching the candlelight play on her face and hair.

At length she fell silent, waiting for him to finish his pie. Making a mental note that she had scarcely touched her food, Jack pushed his plate aside, smiling at her.

"Thank you for the delicious meal. As you could see, I was hungry."

"I'd rather feed a hungry man anytime," she returned graciously.

"You said in your note you wanted to talk with me?"

"Yes—I—I wondered why you pretended you didn't know me there on the street," she began hesitantly. "Have I offended you in some way? Perhaps there on the veranda at Dreyton Hall?"

"I can assure you, Mrs. Dureen, you have not and could not offend me," Jack said, his coolness belying the way he felt inside.

"Then what am I to think, Captain? You left the dance without a word, then pretended you didn't know me there on the street. I thought we were—were friends. Is it because you don't trust me?"

"No," he denied quickly, agonizing over the rest of his answer. "Something that happened a long time ago has placed me in a dangerous situation. People around me could be hurt."

"You came to see John Dreyton. Does this 'dangerous situation,' as you call it, have anything to do with the planters?" Cordelia whispered, her eyes luminous in the dim light.

"Partly. John has been a longtime friend of mine."

"My brother is a planter. Would you like to talk with him? I'm sure I could arrange it."

"Is he having trouble too?"

"He won't talk to me about it. He doesn't want me to worry about such things. But I've heard the workers on the lowlands and the servants whispering about it. He has suffered losses, but I don't know to what extent."

"Mrs. Dureen—"

"You may call me Cordelia, Captain."

"Cordelia," Jack began again, leaning toward her so he could see her face clearly. "Have you ever heard of nightriders?"

"Yes. I've overheard the hired help discussing the term, but when I'd ask them about it, they would look at one another and refuse to talk. They all seem fearful."

"Are you sure you can't recall anything?" he pressed.

"No," she said slowly, a worried expression coming to her face. "Jack, what's happening? My brother has insisted I come into town to live for a while, and he's told me not to ride out to his plantation alone. Is he in danger?" She seemed unaware she had used Jack's first name.

"I don't know, Cordelia. I don't have all the pieces yet, but from what I've heard, there are mysterious nightriders who are destroying crops the planters need to pay off their debts to the bank. When the bank refuses to extend more credit to them, someone steps in to offer a meager price for the land, or the bank forecloses. Someone stands to get very rich."

"I wonder," Cordelia murmured, with a slight frown.

"You wonder?"

"Wilford Crenshaw presses me to marry him every time he sees me. Last night he hinted at something big happening and implied he could give me anything in the world I wanted."

"He said that, did he? How interesting!" Jack mused.

"Little does he know. I wouldn't marry him if he was the last man on earth," she said with spirit. "He's the one who told me you were staying at the inn. He said you were a dangerous man and that I should stay away from you. Has he been by to see you?"

"No. But he could have seen me leave the hotel the other night."

"I don't think so. He stopped at Medford's table to talk for a moment," she answered thoughtfully.

A warning flag went up in Jack's mind. Tom Searles was the only person who had been told where he was staying. Could there be a link between Searles and Crenshaw after all? The two of them working together would stand to gain a lot.

"Cordelia, do you know a Thomas Searles?"

"That horrible man—yes, I know him and detest him! He married a good friend of mine." Tears came to her eyes, and her voice broke as she went on: "Poor Esther—she never should have died. She was so full of life, but he made a slave of her. I think death was her only escape."

"How did she die?"

"Searles said she slipped and fell, hitting her head. He appeared so broken by it all that no one ever questioned his story."

"How long has it been?" Jack asked, trying to appear only mildly curious.

"About three years ago."

There was a pause as Jack thought about this bit of information. Had Esther Searles become a victim of the same cruelty that Tom Searles exhibited toward Mantie?

"I'm sure it's been a terrible loss; it seems she left Mr. Searles pretty well fixed," he commented, fishing for more information.

"That's the shame of it all: Esther's first husband left her very well off," Cordelia replied heatedly, getting to her feet. "But enough of this. It hurts to talk about it. Let's go into the sitting room for coffee."

"You don't speak as a Southerner," Jack observed. Moving to her side, he took note that the dark crown of her head came to the top of his shoulder.

"Nor do you, Captain," she returned, giving him a radiant smile. "I suspect we were both transplanted from the North. My father was a sea captain. He located here to be near the source of goods to be traded at foreign ports. His ship went down in a terrible storm that hit the coast. Mother died a few years ago. And you, Captain?"

"My father came south before the war to get my mother out of the cold winters. Her health was not good. He bought a large farm east of Atlanta and did well. During Sherman's march to the sea, everything he worked for was plundered, burned to the ground, and destroyed. It took its toll on Father, and he died." His voice took on a bitter note. "Betrayed by a Confederate comrade, I rotted in a stench-filled Yankee prison during the war, while Mother died of a broken heart."

Cordelia stopped to look up at him, her eyes full of compassion. "Who did this to you?" she asked tremulously, reaching a sympathetic hand out to touch his arm. She was not prepared for the change that occurred in him.

The warmth left his eyes, and she sensed a coldness come over him. "The same man who is destroying the planters and killing those who get in his way," he said in a tone that sent chills over her.

"Do I have reason to fear him?"

"Yes, he is a traitor and a turncoat, one who thinks only of himself."

"Then my brother is right. It's best for me to remain in Charleston."

Entering the sitting room, she sat down before a tray bearing a server and cups. Jack seated himself opposite her.

"Do you take anything in your coffee?"

"Nothing, please."

"You mentioned your folks were devout Christians. You do not share their faith?"

Jack took a sip of his drink before answering, his handsome face a mask. He had never thought of himself as unchristian—it was just that he did not share the fanatic views of the rest of the family.

"That is a decision each man must make for himself," he said slowly. "It has been my privilege in this life to champion the cause of others, those who cannot help themselves. Religion can make a man weak."

Cordelia stared at the big gun hanging at his hip in its well-worn holster. Suddenly the reason he was here dawned upon her. "You're here to kill that man, aren't you?" Cordelia stated, her face paling.

"Yes—unless he gets me first," Jack answered candidly with a shrug.

"But, Jack, that's murder!"

He set the cup down and got to his feet. "That's what all the self-righteous people say until trouble comes their way; then they call for men like me," he said coldly. "My gun is never pulled unless there is a just cause, and I've never shot a man unless it was to save the life of another or my own. If that makes me a murderer, so be it!"

His reaction stunned her, and it took Cordelia a moment to realize what she had done. Dismayed with herself, she came close to stand before him, her heart pounding in her breast. His eyes bored into hers, and she saw a strange light come into them.

"Jack—," she began, her voice faltering, "I'm sorry—you—misunderstood what I meant." She dropped her head as a crimson tide spread across her face. "It's just that—well, I've grown fond of you, and—and if you kill that man—you'll go to prison."

"Cordelia, what are you saying?" he cried in disbelief, lifting her chin with his hand.

"I am saying, Captain Andrew Jackson Brevard—I love you—," she said softly, with shining eyes, "and I don't want to lose you like I did John."

She heard his gasp and felt his arms close around her. Pressed against his chest, she could hear the rapid beating of his heart.

"Please, for my sake, give up this madness," she pleaded.

She felt him stiffen, and then suddenly he thrust her from him. "You're like all the rest," Jack ground out in disgust. "You play with a man's feelings, talking about love; then you try to make a man less than what he is. You're a selfish, pampered woman, Mrs. Dureen. Now if you would please get my hat, I'll go."

He waited in silence as she brought his hat. Her face was pale, and there were tears in her eyes. Deep within he was pained. He would have much rather kissed her trembling lips than taken his hat and turned to go.

Like a drowning man, he walked to the door, turning to look back at her standing there with her hands outstretched. Lurching outside, he took a long, deep breath of the cool night air.

"Now you've done it," he muttered, jamming his hat onto his head as he headed down the steps.

8

THE SORREL WAS ANXIOUS TO GO, and Jack rode swiftly through the night, grateful the sandy street muted the sound of the horse's movement. He needed to get where he could think clearly.

Jess!—he had forgotten about him. Swerving off to the right toward Meeting Street, he spotted a group of riders coming from his right. He rode into some shadows to wait until they passed. They rounded the corner, talking among themselves, but he couldn't make out what they were saying. However, he recognized the horseman in the lead as Baxter Spriggs.

He waited until they had turned another corner, and then, acting on a hunch, he doubled back, weaving his way to the rear of the stable at Tom Searles's place.

Leaving the sorrel a short distance away, Jack crept through the dark to enter the stall. The horse stood listless and tired, his wet coat bearing evidence he had been ridden hard. A sound outside the door startled Jack. He dropped to the floor and crawled under the horse to fade into the corner.

A strip of light shone under the door, and he heard a grunt as someone pushed on the heavy door. Jack pulled his gun and waited. Light slowly filled the room as the door swung open.

"No cause he had to git a body from bed fer them saddle-bags tonight," a voice mumbled. It was Mantie!

Jack stood up, shoving his revolver in its holster. Frightened, Mantie opened her mouth to cry out, but Jack spoke her name and placed his finger over his lip. Motioning her to close the door, he waited until she complied, then stepped to her side. Her face was badly swollen where she had been struck. Anger welled up in his heart.

"Mantie, do you want to leave here? This is your chance. I can take you to safety."

Big tears welled up in her eyes, and she clung to him.

"Ya won't let him git t' me no more?"

"I promise. Come—we'll have to hurry. Where's those saddlebags?"

"He say over there," she said, pointing to where they hung on the stall behind the horse.

Jack grabbed them and turned out the lantern. Slipping out into the darkness, he heard Searles call from the porch, "Mantie, what's keepin' you? Get yer hide in here! You'll be gettin' another whippin' fer this!"

Jack felt the girl slump against him in fear. He picked her up, surprised at how little she weighed. Running to where the sorrel waited, he stepped into the saddle with the girl still in his arms. Urging the horse forward, they moved silently away in the dark. Behind them he heard Searles roar. Mantie gasped and went limp in his arms.

Once out in the street, he kicked the sorrel into a fast gait and didn't stop until he reached the barn behind Crawfish's house. Jess heard him coming and rushed to open the gate.

"Take the girl, Jess. She needs care. I've got to cover my tracks. Anything around here I could use?"

"Dere's a log o'er dere by de wood pile. You could drag it."

"Lay her down in the barn, Jess, and see if you can find me a rope."

Jess returned with the rope and helped to tie it to the log so Jack could pull it behind him.

"That should do fine, Jess—now see to the girl," Jack whispered hoarsely over his shoulder, taking to his saddle. "I'll be back later."

Pulling the log behind him, Jack swept away the sorrel's tracks far back up the sandy street, then rolled the log over the side of a grassy ditch. He grunted with satisfaction when he heard it splash into unseen water. Hopefully it would float away. Mounting up, he headed back into town, going down by way of the river. Leaving the sorrel at the livery stable, he began the long walk back to where Jess waited.

When he arrived, there was a light burning in the house. Going to the barn, he whispered Jess's name, but there was no answer. Puzzled, he turned his steps to the house. The light had been extinguished, and there was dead silence except for the croaking of a bullfrog in a water ditch.

Treading softly on the porch, he pecked on the door, calling out to Jess. The door swung open, and an arm shot out to pull him in. Jack sensed that there were others in the room.

"It's all righ', Crawfish'; it's de cap'n."

Somewhere a match was struck and held to the wick of a lamp hanging in a bracket on the wall. Lowering the shade, Crawfish blew out the match and discarded it in a can hanging below the lamp.

Other than himself there were four people in the room: Crawfish, Jess, Mantie, and another young girl, whom he had never seen. All eyes were on Jack, wide and questioning.

"There is no way they can trace Mantie," he announced, noticing their obvious relief. "I set up a false trail down by the river and left the horse at the livery stable."

"Mantie done told us what happ'n," Jess stated. "But what I wanna know is what you wuz doin' dere—'n' I wants de truth."

"I had dinner with Mrs. Cordelia Dureen this evening. She had sent a note saying she wanted to talk to me. I went thinking I could learn some valuable information, and I did.

"Upon leaving there, I saw the nightriders coming toward me. Hiding in the shadows, I waited for them to pass. I recognized the leader. Jess, he was the man who booted you down at the market. Name's Baxter Spriggs.

"Acting on a hunch, I circled around and went back to check Tom Searles. He's been letting on to me he's crippled in his legs, and I had reason to suspect he wasn't telling the truth. Since the nightriders were coming from that direction, I had to know if he was in with them. So I went back to check to see if his horse had been ridden lately. I ran into Mantie there. You know the rest."

"Mantie said you is a friend of his," Jess accused.

"We were prisoners together during the war. I really know nothing about him. He sent for me, saying he was in trouble and that our enemy Clemson was here."

Jess was about to speak when Crawfish raised his hand to silence him. Giving Jack a thoughtful look, he nodded his gray head.

"We all 'preciate what ya done fer poor Mantie here, Cap'n, but I reckon it's 'bout time we be gettin' t' sleep. Cally, take Mantie in with ya, and the rest of ya'll are welcome t' the barn. G'night."

"Jess, why are you so cantankerous all the time?" Jack complained, once outdoors. "What's eating you, anyway?"

"You don't think I knows what yer up t'?" Jess exploded. "You be pullin' de wool overn all dere eyes, but I's on t' ya—hobnobbin' with suspicious folks, den actin' like you is our friend."

"Jess, I'm telling you for the last time: you've got to trust me. Just because I'm 'hobnobbin',' as you call it, doesn't mean I'm not on your side. I've got to appear friendly until I find out what they're up to." Jack took hold of Jess's arm, wheeling him around. "I'm laying my own life on the line here. There's more to this than you think!

"Here—sit down here," Jack urged, pushing Jess down onto a stump of wood near the woodpile. "Jess, I believe we're up against something big. I have reason to think there's more than one person masterminding this movement against the planters. Money and power attract evil, greedy men like carrion draws the buzzards. Whoever is the head of those nightriders has an accomplice at the bank.

"Now, my plan is this. I'm going to ride out and talk to some of the planters. I'd like to know who their banker is. Medford does business with Crenshaw's bank. Medford's crops were destroyed, and he can't make payment on his loan. Crenshaw's refused to lend him more money, and he's having the pressure put on him to sell out.

"I'll need to borrow your horse to hunt another for myself. I won't be able use the sorrel anymore, and Prince might be recognized by the nightriders. If that happens, they'll know I'm the man who was at your pa's place that night."

Jess had sat with his head bowed all the while Jack was talking. Now he held his head high, and Jack felt, rather than saw, his deep agitation.

"Cap'n, I's tellin' ya it ain't been easy fer me t' trust no white man. Especially after what's done happened t' m' fam'ly—Pa, Ma, 'n' poor Mantie."

"Mantie?" Jack echoed in surprise.

"Mantie's my sister, Cap'n. I 'preciate ya bringin' her back t' her folks. I wuz gonna go kill dat man Searles, but Mantie say she wuz a hidin' in dat barn ya found her in. I reckon I got cause to 'preciate what ya done fer us."

"You've got a right to be suspicious, Jess. But I'm telling you—my word is good. I'll stand by you. When all this is over—if I live through it—I'd like to have a place of my own. Perhaps you and Mantie will come and work for me. I'll give you a good home and a piece of ground you can call your own." Jack stretched and yawned. "Right now we better get some shut-eye. Mind if I share your hay?"

Tired as he was, when he was stretched out in the hay, Jack found sleep evaded him. His mind refused to put aside the thoughts swirling in it. Long after Jess had fallen into a fitful sleep, Jack lay thinking about what had transpired that day.

It was obvious Mantie had lied to Jess about hiding in Tom Searles's barn because she feared for his life. She knew her brother wouldn't have a chance against the lynch mob who wanted him dead. Jess had said Clemson had taken his sister. If so, how was it she was an unwilling servant for Tom Searles? Lying there, Jack tried to fit the puzzle together. Tom Searles had not been truthful to him, lying about his legs. Mantie had lied to Jess about why she was in Searles's barn. Jack was sure Mantie knew more than she had let on. Poor girl was too filled with fear to talk. If he could win her confidence, perhaps he could get her to open up to him.

Cordelia had hinted of Wilford Crenshaw's involvement in something big. Was he the mastermind behind the whole plan? Jack doubted it. He lacked the fire to lead men. Crenshaw's desire for power and wealth was motivation enough.

Well, tomorrow he and Jess would do some riding. Perhaps the answer lay with the landowners.

*   *   *

Jack rode into town to meet George Medford at the small café on East Bay. Medford was already there, sitting at a table along the wall, and his countenance brightened perceptibly as Jack entered.

Once their order had been taken, both got down to the business of signing the papers, and Jack handed over the money.

"I'll take care of settlin' up at the bank first thing," Medford assured Jack, then added with a laugh, "Won't his eyes bug out, though?"

"And probably a few others," Jack commented with a wry smile. "Which reminds me—do you have enough hands out there?"

"Been shorthanded ever since the nightriders came. The next day the Blacks didn't show, 'n' I can't seem t' get anyone t' work for me. They seem afraid."

"I've got a couple to send you—it's a man and his sister," Jack informed Medford, telling him about Jess and Mantie. "You can give Jess a rifle and let him help ride shotgun on the place. I need him in a strategic place where I can reach him when I need him."

"Fine with me," Medford agreed. "I'll make 'em comfortable."

"Another thing: we're going to need men who'll be willing to face a showdown when the time comes. These people are not going to take kindly to someone exposing them."

"I know of a couple we can trust," Medford interjected eagerly. "I'll check around. There may be more."

"Good! I can't carry this fight alone. Get as many as you can to a meeting at your place two days from now. I'll ride out and meet with you. The planters have got to understand they will never have peace until they stand up to these vermin and clean them out."

"You can count on me, Mr. Brevard," Medford vowed forcibly, fire coming into his hawklike eyes.

"Call me John Blosser for the time being, Medford. It's best they don't know who's backing you. Some of the others may let it slip."

"Blosser it is."

"Make sure you speak to no one of this," Jack reiterated, pushing back his chair to stand.

Medford nodded, getting to his feet. "Like I said, Blosser, I'm a man of my word—you can count on it."

"You're going home after you finish your business?"

"Plan to—right away. My wife'll be worried. Why?"

"Thought I'd send Jess and Mantie out today or tomorrow," Jack replied.

"Anytime. My wife is feelin' poorly, and she'll be glad t' have the help."

Jack raised his hand in farewell and walked out to his horse. He glanced back as he rode away to see Medford emerge from the building to take to his saddle. Jack rode quickly, circling to a vantage point opposite the bank.

In a matter of moments, Medford came into view. Jack gave a satisfied grunt as he watched him dismount and stride into the bank. But still he waited until Medford came out to ride away.

He was just about to leave when he saw Wilford Crenshaw emerge from the bank to hurry off up the street where he entered the door of a brick building. Pulling his hat lower over his face, Jack rode by. A sign over the door read "Otis J. Teasberry, Counselor at Law."

"So the honorable Mr. Teasberry is in on this deal, huh?" Jack muttered under his breath.

He thought about it as he rode out to where Jess was waiting for his return—Baxter Spriggs, Clemson, Wilford Crenshaw, and probably Teasberry. Now he had four names, five counting Searles. But if Searles was in with the nightriders, what about Clemson? It would be inconceivable for Tom Searles to be working with Clemson.

Jess was not in the barn when he arrived. Leaving his horse in the barnyard, Jack went to the house, where he found Jess and Crawfish trying to calm the frantic Mantie, who was in tears, trembling and fearful.

"What's going on?" Jack asked with consternation.

"Ya ain't heared? Dey beat Miz Mary plumb near death tryin' t' make her tell where me 'n' Mantie wuz," Jess informed him. "Mantie's been near out of her haid ever since!"

"Where's my friend Mary now?"

"De neighbor's takin' care of 'er."

"Jess, you take Mantie and ride out to Medford's place. I just talked to him, and he's expecting you. There you'll both have a home and a job. But lay low and stay out of sight."

Turning to Crawfish, Jack addressed the patriarch: "Mantie will need a disguise. Can you rustle up a pair of pants and a shirt? She'll need a hat too. You get her ready. Jess and I will saddle up."

Out in the barn, Jack led Prince from the stall. "Jess, you take my horse for Mantie. I'll ride Prince. Looks like the fat is in the fire anyway."

Jess gave him a questioning glance over the back of his horse. "I gave Medford the money to pay off his debt at the bank. This is not going to play well among the group. Go straight and fast to Medford's," Jack instructed. "You want—umph—to—umph—get in there before dark," he continued between grunts, pulling the cinches tight on his saddle. "Can you shoot?"

"Yes suh!"

"Good! Medford's going to give you a rifle. Use it if you have to. I'm going to ride over to Mary's, then check on another matter. Tell Medford I'll be along later."

Crawfish brought Mantie from the house looking pretty absurd in the big pants and shirt. With the hat pulled low over her face, she would not be easily recognized.

"Take care, Jess," Jack called after them.

"Ya do de same, Cap'n," Jess responded over his shoulder.

Watching until they had vanished from sight, Jack turned to Crawfish. "You've gone beyond the call of duty in helping us, Crawfish. I trust you'll be safe."

"Cap'n, I fought in the war betwixt the states, 'n' I's done learn ya can't run from trouble. There's a time a man's gotta stop 'n' face up. I knows the Lord, Cap'n, 'n' I'd rather meet my Maker doin' what I's gotta do."

Jack felt touched by the man's statement of faith and found himself, for the first time, repeating something his father had said to him many years ago.

"You're right, Crawfish. My father always said the Lord expects a good soldier to put on the whole armor of faith and stand for what's right."

"Yes suh—sometimes when yer soldierin' fer the Lord, yer fightin' yer own battle, sho' 'nuff."

"Well, hold on to your faith, Crawfish; I've got a feeling we're going to win this one," Jack exhorted, climbing into the saddle. "We'll meet again, friend."

Jack rode away surprised at his own response. It had been many years since he had heard his father say those words. Why had they come back to him now? His mind went back to that day when he told his father he had joined the Confederate forces and was leaving for battle.

Standing there so proud in his uniform, he was adamant as his father expressed his disappointment at having a son fight for a cause he abhorred. Seeing his son unmoved, he had begged Jack to take the Lord with him and at least to wear the armor of faith.

"Kneel and pray with me, Son," his father had pled, but Jack had turned a deaf ear, striding to his army conscript horse to mount up and ride off, leaving his father there in the yard.

At the top of the hill he had paused to look back. His mother and younger brother had come to the porch. He had waved his hat at them as a great sense of freedom swept over him. Then with a cry of exhilaration he had ridden away.

Little had he known then he would never see his parents again and that the brother he had loved would die so tragically. What a young fool he had been to think things would go on forever the same—that someday he would come riding back and they would all still be there! In a few tragic years all he had held dear was taken away.

Jack shuddered as a sense of foreboding came over him, and he bowed beneath it. Instinctively, he knew this would be his last battle. When this was over, if he was still alive, he would lay aside the gun that had been so much a part of his life. No more would he ride the lonely trail.

Etched in his memory was a fair face with dark, pleading eyes. "Captain Andrew Jackson Brevard—I love you—and I don't want to lose you." Great remorse filled his heart as he remembered his harsh words. He had spurned her love. Most certainly she would never forgive him for his despicable behavior.

Tormented with conflicting emotions, Jack wound his way through the narrow streets, scarcely aware of where he was going. Only when he reached the Ashley River did he realize he had come too far. Preoccupation could make a man lose his edge and become vulnerable, Colonel Stothard had always told his men. For the first time in his life, Jack felt a sense of premonition come over him, leaving him shaken.

Swinging to the ground, he took stock of what was going on around him, then stood looking westward. Out there, across to the Georgia hills, was the only home he had known. Memories of a happy boyhood crowded into his mind, and with them the day he had turned his back on those he loved most to enter the regimented life of the army. The fighting, the long trails, the camaraderie of the colonel's men had kept away the ghosts of the past.

Now it all returned to haunt him. "They who live by the sword shall die by the sword," his father had said. "Was this to be his last trail? His father, mother, and younger brother were in heaven. That fact he had never doubted. But what about him? Was there a God for a man with blood on his hands and murder in his heart?

The thought struck him forcibly, and he bowed his head in despair. When this was over, he vowed silently, he would return to his home in Georgia. Perhaps there he would find the peace that had eluded him for so long. Like others of the colonel's men, his lonely road was coming to an end, and the time had come to put down his roots. Having made that decision, the dark mood he struggled with lifted.

Prince nuzzled his arm, reminding him it was time to go. Stepping into the saddle, Jack turned his face toward Charleston and the danger that lay ahead. By the time he arrived at Mary's little cottage, he felt like himself again.

Several women were in the room when he entered. Mary, he was told, was in her bed and not able to see anyone.

"She'll see me," Jack said quietly. "Tell her Captain Jack's here."

An older woman disappeared behind a door curtain dividing the two rooms. A moan was heard by those waiting in the outer room, and the woman returned to usher him in.

Propped up in the bed with both eyes swollen shut, Mary was not a pretty sight. Lacerations were evident on her arms, legs, and across her face, where a whip had been applied without mercy. Anger welled up in him.

"Mary, who did this to you?" he asked heatedly, leaning over her.

She whimpered, trying to move her lips where blood had dried in the cuts.

"Don't try to speak, Mary—just nod your head. Did Clemson do this?"

When no answer was forthcoming, he tried again, "Mary, did Baxter Spriggs do this to you?"

Mary groaned and moved her head up and down ever so slightly. A big tear rolled down her cheek.

"Don't you worry none, Mary—I'll take care of it," Jack reassured her, his eyes becoming cold. "The person who did this will pay."

The hurting woman lifted a hand, trying to reach out to him. He touched it gently and lowered it to the bed. Turning away, he followed the older woman from the room.

"Has a doctor seen her?"

"No suh."

"I'll find one and send him out," Jack offered, letting himself out the door.

Once outside, the anger he had kept hidden reached its boiling point. He was sure Tom Searles was behind the attack on this innocent woman. Spriggs must have figured out who Jess was and told Searles he was with Mary. It was natural Searles would think it was Jess who had stolen Mantie away.

Jack mounted Prince and headed for a doctor he had met before when one of the colonel's men had been hurt. When he arrived at the modest building, he was relieved to see a carriage tied at the rail.

An old army man, Doc Steen had stayed in the area to practice, enjoying the privilege of being the only doctor around. But now younger men had moved in, taking a large bite out of his practice. Only the faithful and a lower class of patients continued to come.

A bell on the door jingled as Jack went in, and the portly doctor emerged from behind a white curtain to look at him with kindly blue eyes over the wire-rimmed glasses that had slid down on his nose. He pointed at a chair with a stick he held in his right hand.

"Have a seat, Mister. I'll be with you as soon as I can," he said, pushing his glasses in place with the back of his hand. "I'm about finished settin' this bone."

Jack took a seat in one of the pressed-back chairs lining the wall, and the doctor vanished behind the curtain again.

"Now this should do it, sonny. It'll hold the leg in place 'til it heals."

"Won't it hurt?" Jack heard a boyish voice say.

"Naw, the bone's been set, and this splint will do the trick."

"Will walkin' hurt it?"

"Naw."

"Thanks, Doc! I knew you could fix it."

The curtain was pushed aside, and a small, freckled-faced boy with a shock of red hair came out, holding a puppy.

"My pup's leg was broked, 'n' Doc fixed it!" he exclaimed triumphantly, holding the small dog out for Jack to see.

"Well, son, I'd say that's a right nice job," Jack agreed, stroking the puppy on the head. "Cute little fella."

"Run along now, sonny," Doc Steen urged. "I got another patient."

"It's not me, Doc," Jack told him, after the door had closed behind the boy. "It's someone else I want you to see. You don't remember me, do you? I was here with one of Colonel Stothard's men a few years ago."

"Well, I do declare—sure I do. You're that captain—uh—fella—"

"Jack Brevard," Jack reminded him, extending his hand.

"Yes, yes—that's it. What can I do for you?"

When Jack told him about Mary, a frown formed on his good-natured face. Shaking his tousled gray head, he let out a long sigh.

"There's been some strange things happenin' around here, Cap'n, and it's gettin' bad."

"These men seem to have no conscience, Doc," Jack responded heatedly, "to beat a defenseless, innocent woman like that. She's suffering something awful."

"Where is she? I'll stop by on the way home."

"Thanks, Doc. I'd ride out with you, but I have another matter to take care of."

Jack gave instructions on how to find Mary, leaving some money on the desk. He walked out to find himself face-to-face with Cordelia Dureen. A long, flowing black dress accented her tiny waist and brought out her beauty. Dark eyes widened at the sight of him, and her expression changed to one of genuine concern when she realized he was coming from the doctor's office.

"Jack—Mr. Brevard—is something wrong?"

"Yes," he found himself saying in jest, placing his hand over his heart, "and it hurts something terrible right here."

"Oh, do you mean you have a bad case of indigestion, Captain?" she retorted, choosing to ignore his meaning. "It couldn't be your heart."

Stunned by her inference, Jack responded coolly, bringing heightened color to her cheeks.

"I can assure you, Mrs. Dureen, my heart is well and in the right place." Drawing her aside, he continued in a low voice. "For your information, I was seeing the doctor for my friend Mary. She is the basket weaver down at the market. She was beaten nearly to death last night."

"Oh dear!" Cordelia gasped. "The poor woman—who did it?"

"A man named Baxter Spriggs. I believe him to be one of the nightriders. He was trying to get information from her."

"Is there anything I can do?"

"There are friends there. It's best you don't get involved. It's hard to say to what extent these people will go."

"I'll go with the doctor," she said decisively. "Someone has got to put a stop to this madness."

Her courage struck Jack forcibly, and he felt his heart swell within him.

"Cordelia, when this is all over—," Jack began, but he was interrupted by Doc Steen, who came out at that moment.

"Miss Cordelia—how lovely you look today! I trust you weren't comin' to see me. There's a patient I need to see about—although I assure you I would rather stay and visit with you."

"You can do both, Dr. Steen," Cordelia returned graciously, "because I'm going with you."

The doctor exchanged glances with Jack, who nodded, "Ahem—I see. Of course, I'll be glad to have the company. Come along."

Jack helped her into the buggy, waiting until they had vanished around the corner before mounting up to ride toward Searles's place. It was growing dark, and Searles would be expecting him.

At Jack's knock, the door was opened by a woman who had been hired to replace Mantie.

"I'm here to see Mr. Searles."

The woman nodded and stood back, allowing him to enter. Her face was expressionless as she led him to where Tom

Searles sat in his chair. Instead of the usual blanket over his legs, he had a light cover over his feet.

"Jack!" Tom Searles greeted him. "What'd you find out?"

Jack stood with his back to the light so he could see Searles clearly. It was important to watch a man's eyes as he talked.

"Evening, Tom—I see your legs are better," Jack noted.

"No better," Tom groaned, his heavy lids lowering to cover his eyes but not before Jack saw a guarded expression come into them.

"Some days they're so bad I can't stand that heavy blanket; this is one o' them days," Searles explained. He looked up. "You hungry?"

"No—can't stay that long. I just came by to tell you I'm going after Clemson. Be gone for several days."

"Good!" Searles responded. "It's about time you got that rotten, low-down traitor."

Jack looked around the room. "Where's Mantie? Is she sick?"

"Up and run away," Searles growled. "Don't know why, after all I've done fer her."

Jack felt a surge of anger and lowered his gaze. He studied a cockroach crawling across the floor while pondering what to say next. Instinctively, he knew this was the last time he would stand in this man's presence without his gun drawn. The roach found a place of refuge at the edge of a rug, remaining motionless. When Jack looked up, Tom Searles was watching him curiously. There was a strange glint in his eyes.

"You always was a deep one, Jack. Wha'cha thinkin' about?"

"I always get moody when I'm about to kill a man," Jack answered coolly.

Searles struck a match and held it to the end of his cigar with a trembling hand. Puffing away, he gave Jack a measured look. "Yeah, I know wha'cha mean. I've felt thataway a few times. It'll wear off," he concluded, blowing smoke into the air.

Leaning forward, he made an attempt at tossing the spent match into the grate. It fell far short of its goal to join others laying in mute evidence of other misses.

"Well, when it's finished, I'll not be sticking around these parts, Tom—I'll be riding on," Jack told him, starting for the door.

"How will I know it's over?"

"You'll know," Jack said grimly and walked out.

Jack mounted Prince and galloped away. There was no doubt in his mind he would be followed. The gauntlet between Searles and himself had been thrown. Searles meant to kill him. Of that he was sure. By now they would have seen him on Prince and known who he was. Every dark corner he passed made the hair stand up on the back of his neck, but he had to keep moving. Winding his way through the streets, he went back to the inn where he had been staying. Perhaps he could give them the slip there.

Leaving Prince in the back, Jack entered the inn through the rear and went to the desk.

"Any messages for John Blosser?" he asked the clerk, turning his back to the desk.

"No sir, Mr. Blosser."

Jack paid little attention to the answer, for at that moment a man with dark visage strolled in to pick up a newspaper and sit down to read. The clerk had become noticeably nervous, putting in the appearance of being busy, shuffling some papers before him.

Jack turned away to mount the stairs calmly. Once in the upper hall, he pulled off his boots and ran down the hall, carrying them in his hand. Slipping quietly down the back stairs, he ran to where he had left Prince. The big horse sensed his owner's urgency and moved out as Jack sprang into the saddle.

By the time they figured out his ruse, he should have a good start on them. A shadow moved in the darkness to his right, and Jack saw the burst of flame as the gun went off. Something caught at his shirt and Jack felt the burn of the bullet in his chest.

"Go, Prince!" he cried, drawing his revolver. He sent two shots in the direction where the bullet had come from and heard a howl of pain. The big horse stretched out in a full gallop, and every beat of his hooves seemed like a sledgehammer going off in his brain. Jack could feel the hot blood running down his chest. Pressing his hand over the wound, he rode toward Mary's. Hopefully Doc would still be there. The last thing he remembered was Cordelia's cry as he fell from the saddle.

9

CONSCIOUSNESS RETURNED like a roaring freight train in his head. When he came to the realization that he was alive and lying on his back, Jack could hear a sound off to his right. Opening his eyes, he saw he was in a room with high ceilings; the bed he was in had four large posts.

He tried to raise himself up, but the effort caused unbearable pain and sent the room spinning. Jack dropped his head back onto the pillow, closing his eyes until his head felt straight. He heard a gasp and felt a cool hand on his forehead. Opening his eyes again, he saw it was Cordelia.

"Don't try to move," she warned with alarm. "You'll cause your wound to bleed. Your fever's broken."

"Where—am—I?" he whispered, letting his gaze roam the room. His clothes were not in sight, but his gun belt hung on a chair.

"You're here in my home. I've been taking care of you."

"What—happened?"

"You were shot. The doctor and I were leaving Mary's when we heard you coming and saw you fall from your horse. We brought you here."

"Prince?"

"Don't worry. He's being cared for. A man by the name of Crawfish has him."

"I—mus'—go," he said, trying to raise up again.

Cordelia gently restrained him. "No, you mustn't! You've had a close call. If you move now, it'll kill you. You're safe. No one knows you're here. We brought you here in Dr. Steen's carriage."

"They'll—know."

"Jack, who did this to you?"

"Couldn't—see" was his weak reply.

"You rest now while I get some broth for you," Cordelia urged, brushing his hair away from his face. "I'll be back in a moment."

Jack closed his eyes, listening to her departing footsteps. As weakened as he was from fever and loss of blood, there was little he could do but be patient.

Jess! He would be worried, as well as Medford. Perhaps Crawfish could get word to them, he determined silently.

Hearing a sound at the door, he opened his eyes to see Cordelia returning with a cup in her hand.

"Good! You're still awake. Let's see how you enjoy this. It's the first you've eaten in four days." She pulled over a chair.

The smell of the broth was nauseating, but Jack knew he would need to eat something to get his strength back. Each time she held a spoon to his lips he slowly sipped the liquid from it, his eyes studying her face.

Cordelia felt the warmth rush to her face, and she avoided his gaze, pretending to be busy with his feeding. His grateful stare reminded her of the time she had removed a sandspur from the foot of a puppy.

"There—that's probably enough for now," she said finally, setting the cup aside. "You can have some more later. You'll need to rest now. Would you like me to read to you?"

Jack nodded his head weakly. It was so good to have her near him that he would have agreed to anything. He wasn't even dismayed when she picked up the Bible she had been reading.

"I was reading in Romans—I'll finish that first," Cordelia said.

Jack watched the light shining on her hair as she read, his eyes growing heavy. The last words he heard played over and

over in his mind as he drifted into sleep—"Vengeance is mine;
I will repay, saith the Lord."

How long he had slept Jack did not know. When he awakened, the sun was casting long shafts of light into the room,
and the chair beside his bed was empty. Listening intently, he
could hear Cordelia's voice as she talked to someone in the hall
below. It was a man's voice that answered. Soon he heard footsteps on the stairs. He looked longingly at his gun and holster
still hanging on the chair.

He struggled to raise himself to a sitting position, but the
pain was so intense he fell across the bed, groaning. Sweat
broke out on his brow. Friend or enemy, it was all the same. He
could do nothing to help himself.

Cordelia was the first one in the door, and she cried out
when she saw him: "Jack, what have you done?"

Grabbing up a cloth, she wet it and bathed his face. Behind her he could see Medford's concerned face.

"You mustn't move," she scolded. "Mr. Medford, help me
get him back on his pillow. There! That should do it. Thank
you!"

Cordelia stepped back near where his gun hung on the
chair, allowing Medford to remain near the bed. Her action,
not lost on Jack, went unnoticed by his visitor.

"Captain Brevard, Mr. Medford says he's a business part-
ner of yours and that you would want to see him. I told him
you were too weak, but he insisted."

"It's—all right, Cor—uh—Mrs. Dureen. What he says—is
true." Looking at Medford, he asked, "Jess—and Mantie?"

"They made it safe enough, Captain. We was worried
when ya didn't show up, though. Then Crawfish sent word
you'd been shot real bad. I'd already figgered t' ride in t' check
on ya. Glad t' see you're makin' it. Miz Dureen says ya had a
close call. Don't 'spose ya know who done it?"

"It was—dark but I have—my suspicions," Jack replied,
grimacing with pain.

"You just lay quiet. I'll do the talkin'. The way Jess 'n' I figger it, things are about t' bust loose any day. That new fella that just built that fancy new home had his cotton set on fire last night. Lost the whole field. They're workin' on him now. He says some shots were fired 'n' one of his workers was killed. I sure hope ya get well a'fore this thin' comes t' a head.

"I'll tell ya one thin'—anybody comin' 'roun' my house is gonna get shot first 'n' questioned afterward," Medford added with a knowing look. "Well, hurry 'n' get well, Captain. I gotta get along."

Cordelia followed Medford downstairs. Jack heard the murmur of their voices but was unable to make out anything being said. When she returned later with a bowl of broth, he noticed she seemed preoccupied and worried. Watching her, Jack remembered Medford's words about the planter near him. Would that have been her brother? He had just built a new home in the area.

"Your brother?" he whispered, before sipping the spoon of broth she held out to him.

Tears sprang to her eyes, and she nodded. Jack could do no more to comfort her than to lift his hand to touch her cheek. When he did, it unleashed all the pent-up emotion she had been hiding, and great sobs racked her body. Setting the soup aside, Cordelia grasped his hand and held it to her lips.

"I—almost lost you and—now this," she stammered, her tears wetting his hand.

"Cordelia—I—"

"Sssh!" she cautioned, lifting her head to listen. There was the sound of horses in the street below, then a loud rap on the door. Jumping to her feet, Cordelia hastened to the window to look out. There was a group of horsemen below, some still sitting on their horses, while others had dismounted and were heading for the house.

"Don't make a sound," she warned, heading for the door. "I'll be back."

"Cordelia, my—gun! Give it—to me," Jack managed.

"Please, Jack—don't try to get up," she whispered, handing it to him. "I'll get rid of them somehow."

The knock came again, and Cordelia left the room, locking the door behind her. Jack buried his holster under the covers, pulling the gun from the sheath to hold unseen in his hand. He waited, straining his ears to catch what was being said.

Cordelia was coming slowly down the stairs when Hettie opened the door. It was Wilford Crenshaw who entered first, and he stepped forward to meet her at the bottom of the steps.

"Cordelia, these men seem to think you have a murderer hiding on the premises." Crenshaw addressed her in a conciliatory tone. "I told them the idea was preposterous. But they have insisted on coming to search the house."

Cordelia had always disliked the way his voice took on a higher pitch when he became excited. She looked over his head, with calm, wide-eyed innocence at the men who were crowding the doorway behind him.

"Gentlemen, may I ask you by whose authority you are pursuing this outrage? I am a respected widow in this community and would have no reason to be a party to such a thing."

One man pushed his way through the group to face her. Two big revolvers swung at his hips, and instinctively she knew this man was Jack's enemy. Narrowed gray eyes coldly appraised her slender form from head to toe. When his gaze returned to hers, Cordelia saw tiny pinpoints of light appear, and his cruel mouth broke into a crooked, sardonic smile. She faced him bravely, an inner calm coming to her rescue as she waited for him to speak.

"Ma'am, we know he's here. Doc Steen's done told us."

"Doc—Dr. Steen?" she stammered in bewildered pretense.

"He said he treated a man for a gunshot wound and brought him here."

"Here? He must be mistaken. A woman living alone must be careful. It would be unthinkable to jeopardize my safety by harboring a—a murderer, now wouldn't it?" she replied with spirit, turning to Crenshaw. "Mr. Crenshaw has known me for a long time, sir. He knows I am not a person to take such risks."

"That's right, Spriggs," Crenshaw gallantly spoke up in her defense.

Spriggs shifted his position to the other foot. His cold glance swept the room, taking in the stairs leading to the upper floor. Cordelia saw he was not convinced and held her breath. One of the men shouldered his way through the door.

"Spriggs, there's no sign of blood or footprints aroun'."

"There! I told you I had nothing to hide. Good day, gentlemen," Cordelia declared, turning her back on them to ascend the stairs. Behind her she heard the shuffling of feet as the men began to leave.

"Go on, Spriggs. I'll be there in a minute," she heard Wilford Crenshaw say.

"Cordelia, wait!"

She turned to see Crenshaw standing at the bottom of the steps. Remaining where she was, Cordelia waited for him to go on.

"Cordelia, I'm sorry about what's happened. I told Spriggs you were not the kind of woman who would be involved in something like this, but he insisted on coming anyway."

"Thank you, Mr. Crenshaw."

"Would you have dinner with me tonight?" he asked hopefully.

"Please excuse me," Cordelia answered, raising a hand to her forehead. "This whole affair has been very upsetting and has given me a horrible headache."

"Of course, my dear. Perhaps soon?"

"Perhaps."

Cordelia continued on her way, listening with relief as he left. Only then did she give in to the weakness that had threatened to overtake her in her confrontation with Baxter Spriggs. Now there is a man to be reckoned with, she thought.

Going to her room where she could look down into the street, she saw Crenshaw mount up to ride out after the rest.

While she watched, Cordelia saw him catch up with the group and come alongside Spriggs. The two men exchanged comments, and there was a shout of laughter. Turning away from the window, she intuitively knew it was more than happenstance Crenshaw was riding with Baxter Spriggs.

Lying there, listening and wondering, Jack detected the sound of hurried footsteps in the hall. He pulled the hammer back on his revolver and pointed the barrel chest high at the door.

"Jack, it's all right," Cordelia exclaimed, bursting through the door. She stopped dead, and her face blanched when she saw the gun pointed right at her.

Jack's hand trembled and went limp. Releasing the trigger, he laid it by his side and reached out to her.

"I'm sorry," he said hoarsely. "I—I didn't know who—it was."

"It must have been dreadful, lying here helpless, knowing your enemies were downstairs," Cordelia said.

"Who was it?"

"A man named Baxter Spriggs and his cohorts; Wilford Crenshaw was with them too," she informed him, telling him all that had happened. "Jack, I suspect Crenshaw is in with these men."

"I believe you're right," Jack agreed. Then he told her all he had observed, leading up to the night he was shot. "Poor Doc—they probably treated him like they did Mary, and by bringing me here you've placed yourself in danger as well. Somehow I must leave as soon as I'm able."

"You can't! If you open your wound again, Dr. Steen says it will kill you!" She brought his hand to her cheek. "Don't worry about me—we'll go through this together. Certainly God will come to our aid. You do believe that, don't you, Jack?"

"I've heard my father say that," he said presently, his voice growing tired. "I'm—not sure—what I believe."

Cordelia placed his hand by his side. His eyes had already grown heavy, and soon he was sound asleep. Slipping quietly away, she left the door open so she could hear his call and went in search of Hettie, locking the front door as she passed.

"Hettie?"

"I's in here, Miz Cordelia."

"Hettie," Cordelia instructed when she came into the pantry where she was. "I want you to keep the doors locked at all times, starting right now. I locked the front door. If those men get to Captain Brevard, they'll kill him. Do you understand? We must not let that happen. He's not able to defend himself."

"Yes'um, Miz Cordelia—I knows," Hettie answered, straightening up. "I done heared 'bout him."

Cordelia stared at her maid in surprise. "What have you heard about him?"

"Thet he's a good man," Hettie replied, eyes growing wide in her round face. "Folks say he's helpin' us."

"You're right, Hettie," Cordelia responded warmly. "The captain is a good man, and we must protect him until he is able to look after himself. Don't forget about the doors."

Leaving Hettie to her work, Cordelia went back upstairs to look in on her patient. He was sound asleep. Wearily, she headed to her room for some much-needed rest. The long nights spent at the bedside of her patient had taken their toll. She fell asleep immediately.

Sometime later, Hettie came to check on them. Nodding her head, she muttered to herself, "Sleep good. They'll both feel better."

It was growing late when Cordelia opened her eyes to find Hettie had lit the lamp on the table. She slipped to her feet and went to find Jack awake, watching the door.

"I'm sorry. I went to my room to rest and fell asleep. Is there anything I can get you?"

"Your maid has been here," he assured her with a wan smile.

"Your voice sounds stronger. You're better. I need to take a look at your wound."

Cordelia removed the bandages to find much of the angry color was gone and the wound closing nicely.

"I'll leave it open to the air while I get some warm water to bathe it before putting clean bandages on," she said, leaving the room.

Jack's gaze was disturbing while Cordelia worked over him. She avoided looking directly at him, her fingers trembling as she worked. When she was finally done and had set the basin aside, she stepped back.

"There! That should make you feel a lot better. Perhaps you'll be able to sit up a little tomorrow. Now, are you hungry?"

"Yes."

"Hettie will be here soon with some soup."

"Sit down, Cordelia. I need to talk with you."

Cordelia seated herself, waiting expectantly as Jack stared at the ceiling for a moment.

"It's been wrong for me to bring my trouble upon you. As soon as I'm able to ride, I must leave—"

"You can't!" Cordelia interrupted. "They're watching the house. They'll kill you!"

"You don't understand—I have a job to do," Jack returned, his voice becoming cold. "The man who's responsible for all this must be stopped. Innocent people are being hurt. You may be next. Not even Wilford Crenshaw can save you if they come after you. Oh, they won't come after you here and drag you into the street. They'll bide their time, catch you out somewhere, and make it look like an accident."

"Surely you're mistaken," she gasped in disbelief.

"These are the same men who tried to burn me to death when I hid Jess to keep him from being lynched, and the same bunch who beat poor Mary near to death. They're ruthless. Only God knows what they did to Doc Steen," Jack reminded her bluntly.

"Jack," she pleaded. "You don't have to be the one to settle this score."

"If a man runs from his trouble, he ceases to be a man. Then he must keep on running, for there will always be men like these in the world. It's my fight, not yours!"

"Then go ahead and throw your life away!" Cordelia cried, fleeing the room.

It was Hettie who brought the soup and fed him. Cordelia did not put in an appearance. The next morning Jack felt more like himself. When Hettie brought his breakfast, he was clearly disappointed. Cordelia had not come in to see him, and he lay listening for her footsteps in the hall outside his door or her voice downstairs.

"Where's Mrs. Dureen?" Jack asked, when Hettie came to get his dishes."

"Miz Cordelia go see 'bout Doc Steen. Say keep yo' quiet."

"Hettie, is the house being watched?"

"Yas suh, Cap'n—I's seen 'em out front," Hettie answered scornfully, "lookin' like a cat waitin' on a mouse. What we needs 'roun' here is a cat trap."

"Maybe I'm just the one to set the trap, Hettie," Jack responded, smiling up at her.

"All us hopin' so, Cap'n. First off, yo' gotta mend."

"What's out back?"

"A big ol' wall. They'd have t' straddle thet iffen they was gonna look down over here," she answered, gathering the dishes onto a tray she was holding.

"How high is the wall?" Jack asked, trying to appear casual.

"Well, suh, it'd take a purty good man t' climb it."

"What's on the other side?"

"Someone else's yard, I reckon," she answered. Placing a hand on her hip, she eyed him suspiciously. "Why yo' axin' all these questuns? Miz Cordelia don't want yo' goin' nowheres."

"No reason, Hettie. I was just wondering what it would take for a man to come after me through that way."

Hettie gave him a strange look and left him. Whatever she was thinking she kept to herself. After she had gone, Jack lay thinking of a plan. If there was some way he could get over the wall, he just might get away.

Taking his pillow, he held it tightly against his chest and tried to sit up. Pain shot through his chest, causing him to break out with sweat. But still he persisted until he was sitting on the side of the bed. The lightheadedness he felt soon passed, and he struggled to his feet to stand there, swaying like a drunken man. Realizing there was no way he could make it to the window, he gave up, vowing to keep repeating the effort until he gained his strength.

Jack's knees buckled beneath him, and he sank down on the bed. He had just made it into a horizontal position when he heard a light step on the stairs. Pretending to be asleep, Jack felt Cordelia's presence beside the bed. No longer able to keep up the charade, he opened his eyes to see her there looking down at him. She must have just come in, for she was still wearing her hat. Dressed in a spring-green dress with a lace bodice insert, she was beautiful.

"I thought you were asleep," she said guardedly.

"I was resting," Jack was able to answer truthfully, after the exertion he had gone through. "Hettie told me you had gone to see about Doc Steen."

"That and some other things; I told Wilford Crenshaw I would have dinner with him tomorrow night," she informed him, watching for his reaction.

"How was Doc Steen?" Jack asked coolly, choosing to ignore the reference to Crenshaw and struggling to control the anger that welled up in him.

"His face was all bruised, and he moved like a man who was sore. He said his buggy hit a rough place in the road one night and he was thrown out. I don't believe his story for a minute."

"He's afraid to talk," Jack responded darkly.

"Is there anything I can get for you before I go to change my clothes?" Cordelia asked, turning toward the door.

"Nothing, thank you."

"You have eaten?"

"Yes."

Cordelia hesitated as if to say something more, then changed her mind. Removing her hat, she turned to leave.

"So after all your sweet talk, you've decided to go back to having dinner with that weasel, Crenshaw," Jack said gruffly.

Cordelia spun around to give him an incredulous look. When the meaning of his words sunk in fully, a rush of color came to her cheeks, and she raised her chin. "And what business is it of yours, may I ask?"

"None really—I'm sorry I asked," he responded bitterly, turning his face away.

After a moment's hesitation, she was gone, closing the door behind her. Had Jack been able, he would have kicked himself. If he had resented her making any demands on him, then why was he interfering with her life? After all, he argued silently with himself, he was but a guest in her home and a recipient of her kindness. Her confession of love was probably born out of infatuation and pity, he jealously reasoned. She would get over it. Wasn't that the way he wanted it?

Between naps, Jack watched the door hopefully, but Cordelia did not come to check on him the rest of the day. It was Hettie who saw to his needs and brought his food. After she had come to remove his supper plate and the house had grown still, Jack forced himself to his feet again. This time he felt stronger. Taking a few steps around the bed, he grunted with satisfaction at his progress, although he was ready when the time came to lie down again.

Awake at dawn the next morning, Jack lay listening to the sounds around him. Other than the song of a mockingbird outside his window, he could not detect anyone moving around.

Pushing off the bed again, he found himself much stronger. Though his chest was sore, the pain accompanying the movement was not as severe as before. He walked around the bed with greater ease.

Back in bed, he lay thinking. It would be only a matter of time before they came for him. Tonight was the night. While Cordelia was out, he would leave.

Somehow he would have to get word to Crawfish to meet him after dark. Hettie was his only hope. When she brought his breakfast, he would have to take her into his confidence, trusting she would not reveal his plan to her mistress.

By the time Hettie came, Jack had taken several walks around the room. His talk with her went well. She was quick to see he must go, especially when he convinced her it was putting their lives at risk.

"Yes suh—I don't mind gettin' word t' ol' Crawfish. He's a brave one. There's a boy comin' by t' do some yardwork. He can go."

"You won't say anything to Miss Cordelia, will you? She might say something to that Crenshaw fella. No one must know. It'll be our little secret."

"No suh—I ain't sayin' nuttin, Cap'n—no suh!" Hettie assured him, her face breaking into a smile. She started for the door, then turned back to come close to his bed.

"Cap'n, is yo' gonna kill thet man what's beat up on poor Mary?" she whispered.

"Baxter Spriggs?"

"No, thet ain't him. I's talkin' 'bout thet other fella."

"Oh, him," Jack replied, his eyes turning cold. "Soon, Hettie. There's only one way to kill a snake. You cut off its head. I'm going to get rid of the man behind this or be killed trying," Jack responded in a low voice.

"Cap'n, suh, is it a'right iffen I say a prayer fer yo'?" Hettie's eyes were filled with compassion as she looked down at him. "Ain't nobody tried t' hep us 'ceptin' Mr. Lincoln, God res' his soul."

Jack was deeply moved by her comment, and warmth surged through his heart. "Yes, Hettie, it's all right if you pray for me—Lord knows I'm going to need all the help I can get," he said gravely.

After she had gone, Jack lay thinking about what lay ahead. Would this be his last cognizant day on this earth? One bullet in the darkness could end his life this time.

His thoughts were interrupted by hurried footsteps, which he had come to recognize as Cordelia's, in the hall. He watched the door, hopeful she would stop in to see him, but the whole day passed without her coming. It was just as well, he thought grimly—it would make his leaving easier.

When Hettie brought his supper, she told him Crawfish would be waiting for him in the trees down by the river. Jack received this information with a nod of satisfaction.

"Hettie, has Mrs. Dureen left yet?"

"Oh, she been gone a long time, Cap'n. She was gonna take a ride 'n de country with Mr. Crenshaw first 'n' have dinner after they get back. Miz Cordelia 'lowed them men wouldn't be so 'spicious iffen she went out some."

Hettie's words struck remorse to Jack's soul and fear in his heart. Cordelia was seeing Crenshaw to buy time for his healing, and all he had succeeded in doing was act like a jealous fool. Though she realized the danger she was putting herself in, she was doing it for him.

"Did she say where they were going?"

"No suh—she sho' didn't," Hettie said over her shoulder.

Jack lost his appetite for the food Hettie had brought but forced himself to eat, knowing he would need all the strength he could get. When Hettie came for his dishes later, she went to the chifferobe and brought out his clothes. The shirt he had been wearing when he was shot had been cleaned and patched.

"While yo' is gettin' dressed," she said, "I's gonna take care of these dishes, then be back to help yo' down the steps."

Getting dressed took a lot of effort, the boots being the worst. But at length he managed, then strapped on his gun belt. To loosen up his legs a little, Jack walked around the room, stopping to peer through the curtains of the front window. In the remaining dim light he could see a man across the street digging into his tobacco pouch for a chew.

Jack grunted as he recognized him. He was the same individual who had ogled Prince out at the shanty that stormy night, which seemed so long ago. To preserve his strength, he went back to bed to wait for Hettie. It would soon be da.к enough to start. It was then he remembered to check his gun, replacing the spent shells fired the night he was shot.

Hurried steps sounded on the stairs. "Cap'n, you gotta hurry," Hettie cried, breathing heavily from her exertion. "They's men ridin' up out front—hurry!"

Even with Hettie's help, it was not an easy task for Jack to descend the stairs. Every step jarred through his whole body. Shuffling feet could be heard on the path outside as Hettie hurried him through the house to the kitchen door.

"Stall them, Hettie, as long as you can," Jack whispered from the dark, squeezing her hand. "Now's when I need that prayer!"

"We both do, Cap'n" was her quiet response as a heavy fist pounded on the front door.

Jack slipped into the night, easily locating the ladder Hettie had left for him at the end of the path. Placing it against the wall, he managed to make it slowly to the top, pushing himself up with his legs to avoid the pain in his chest. He gave the ladder a shove sideways, and it fell with a soft thud on the ground.

Standing there on the wall, panting from exertion, he knew he was committed. His only way down was to jump. He paused a moment, studying the ground on the other side of the wall in the dim light. Below him was what appeared to be a vegetable garden. The tilled soil would best break his fall, he decided. Hettie's screams were all it took to propel him over the side.

Placing his hand tightly over his wound, Jack jumped, hitting the soft dirt. His legs buckled beneath him, and he fell sideways into a patch of cabbage. Pain shot through his chest, and he laid there gasping for breath, fighting to remain conscious. Struggling to his feet, he moved on.

A soft light shone deep in the recesses of the house looming over him in darkness. Twenty feet off to the side was a gate leading to the street. Jack headed for it and lifted the latch. The gate swung open, its rusty hinges objecting to use.

Aroused by the noise, a dog in the yard next door began barking furiously. Without hesitation, Jack slipped through the aperture, expecting the back door to open any moment.

Gaining the street, he kept to the deeper shadows, making his way toward the river. Back of him he heard shouts, and he knew there was precious little time to find Crawfish.

Crawfish must have heard the noise, for he came riding toward him from the shadows with Prince in tow.

"No time t' be wastin', Cap'n. Climb up 'n' we'll ride!" he called softly.

"Need help," Jack panted, holding his chest. Each breath he took was like fire in his lungs.

Crawfish swung from the mule he was riding and almost effortlessly shoved Jack aboard Prince. Then they faded into the shadows of the tree-lined dirt road. Jack swayed weakly in the saddle and would have fallen except for the black man's steadying hand.

To Jack the ride seemed interminably long, and he was growing faint when Prince came to a halt. Strong hands drug him from the saddle, and he heard soft whispers as he was half led, half carried into a house and put onto a bed. Shadowy figures worked over him, and he felt warm hands touching his chest.

"Aw, dat's good—he ain't a bleedin'; jest plum tuckered from all de c'motion," a voice over him said quietly. It was Mose. Jack felt himself drifting off into a deep sleep.

*C*ORDELIA AWAKENED to the sound of voices in the next room, but she could not make out what was being said. The smell of breakfast was in the air, and no doubt Hettie had brought food to their patient.

She stretched long and hard, dreading to face the day, wishing she had not accepted the invitation to have supper with Wilford Crenshaw. Yet for her patient's sake she must keep up the appearance of normalcy.

She lay there thinking over the last couple of days. It seemed that in spite of her pleas Jack was determined to go after the enemy he had sought for so long. According to him, the same man was responsible for all the terrible things happening in the area. In spite of her fear for his safety, Cordelia knew in her heart he was right.

Her thoughts returned to his remark about Crenshaw, and she smarted at his insinuation. Hurt at first when he had ignored the news she was seeing Wilford, she was too proud to let him know it was for his sake. Stung by his cryptic response, she had run from his presence, vowing to avoid him. Her anger soon cooled, however, when she realized he probably was jealous of Crenshaw.

In spite of his actions, Cordelia believed Jack cared for her—she saw it in his eyes. Since there was no way she could stop him from doing the murderous deed he was undertaking, she decided she could only pray God would change his mind.

Well, she would just let him miss her again today, she thought, slipping out of the covers—then she would look in on him in the morning. Perhaps she could learn something from Crenshaw, and Jack would be pleased when she brought him news.

Donning a robe and slippers, Cordelia went downstairs to see what Hettie had fixed for breakfast. The morning was spent in catching up on some correspondence. Then she went upstairs to slip into a modest brown dress with a matching hat and veil. There would just be time to go to the post office before meeting Wilford at the bank.

Crenshaw was waiting for her in his office, and his eyes lit up, as they always did, at the sight of her. "My, but you look lovely today, Cordelia!" he exclaimed, coming around his desk. "It's going to be a nice day for our ride."

He took Cordelia's extended hand in his, peering at her more closely. "You look tired; have you been ill?"

"Not ill—just worried about my brother," she answered evasively. "I've been lying awake nights thinking about him. Have you heard any word of his welfare?"

"No, can't say I have," Crenshaw responded guardedly, turning to reach for his hat on the hall tree. "But I've been quite busy and haven't been in on the outer-office gossip. Shall we go?"

Cordelia took the arm he offered. Wilford Crenshaw had never been a good liar. His eyes always betrayed him. She gave him a disarming smile as they waited for the carriage he had ordered, very much aware of the game she was playing.

A black carriage with gold trim rounded the corner, pulled by a sleek black horse. "Ah, here we are!" Wilford exclaimed importantly as the driver pulled to a stop before them. "May I help you, my dear?"

Cordelia allowed him to assist her, and when they were seated, he gave the driver instructions to James Island.

"That's so far, Wilford," Cordelia protested.

"It's lovely out on James Island this time of year now that the summer heat's over," Crenshaw said, settling back in his seat. "I thought we'd drive out that way."

In spite of the situation, Cordelia found the open air invigorating. On the other side of the Ashley, she leaned back to enjoy the countryside lined with huge live oak trees mingled with pine. Crenshaw kept up a lively chatter about events around town, but before long Cordelia noticed he seemed watchful and somewhat nervous. Soon he fell silent.

"Cordelia, I—," he began then seemed to change his mind.

"What is it, Wilford?"

"It was nothing," he replied, pulling at his collar as if it were too tight.

"Are you all right?"

"Oh, I'm fine. Just warm, that's all.

"You just seem so nervous all of a sudden," she observed.

She did not see the masked riders come from the trees ahead to turn into the road, coming toward them. Not until the carriage came to a sudden halt and the driver stepped down did Cordelia realize what was happening. Brandishing their guns, the riders encircled them. One was holding the reins of an extra horse.

"What is the meaning of this?" she cried, turning to Crenshaw. "Wilford, what—?"

When she saw his face, she knew the truth. He was part of a carefully laid plan, and she had allowed herself to fall into their trap. Her heart froze in fear—not for herself, but for Hettie and Jack lying helpless back at the house. By not heeding Jack's warning, she had placed them both in grave danger.

"Step out of the carriage, ma'am," the masked leader ordered.

"I will not," Cordelia said with all the bravado she could muster. "Wilford, take me back to town this minute."

The masked man rode his horse nearer to grasp her arm and pulled her out. Cordelia screamed and tried to wrench her arm free, but it was no use. He was too strong.

Still, she continued to struggle. "Crenshaw, take the reins and get that buggy out of here," the man yelled, dropping the reins to free his left hand.

As Crenshaw jumped to obey, Cordelia bit her captor's arm. He swore, flinging her unceremoniously to the ground. In the melee, her hat was jarred from her head to fall in a clump of weeds by the road, and her hair fell around her shoulders.

"Wilford, don't leave me here with these men!" she screamed after him, tugging at her dress to pull it over her legs. Ignoring her cries, he turned the carriage and drove swiftly away without looking back. Even as she saw him go, Cordelia knew he was a marked man.

"Bring that horse over here," the leader ordered.

The masked rider complied, then picked up Cordelia roughly and shoved her onto the saddle. Though the brown dress she wore was fairly full, still it could not hide her shapely legs from the leering eyes of the men.

Someone from behind tied a handkerchief over her eyes, then flipped the animal with the reins. The horse started forward so suddenly it almost unseated her. Cordelia grabbed the saddle horn for balance.

No one saw the dark figure of a young man peering from behind the big oak tree. When the strange procession passed out of sight, he stepped cautiously into the road to take a close look at the tracks. He stared at the trail of dust in the distance, shaking his head sadly.

"Somethin' bad's happenin'," he muttered, scanning the area with fearful eyes. "No black man better be found 'round here." Moving noiselessly off into the bush, the man broke into a run and did not stop until he had reached the river. Taking a small rowboat, he made his way to the opposite shore, where he secured the boat and faded into the dusty streets of Charleston.

*   *   *

Unable to see, Cordelia listened to every sound that might serve as a clue to where she was being taken. But other than the noise of the horses, the creaking of leather, and a few grunts from the men, the ride was made in silence. The sound of night creatures had already started a steady rhythm when her horse came to a stop.

"Go in 'n' light a lamp," a voice she had come to recognize as belonging to the leader instructed.

Rough hands pulled her from the saddle, and she was led up on a wooden porch. When she hesitated, a hand from behind pushed her forward. Once inside, there was the smell of kerosene and the sound of a match being struck. A door opened to her right, and she was shoved in that direction.

"Behave yersef, 'n' I won't hafta tie ya up," her captor said, turning the key in the lock. His footsteps faded into the other room. Something was said, and there was an outburst of laughter.

Cordelia tore the blindfold from her eyes to find she was in a small room with the lone window boarded up. There was just enough of the waning daylight coming through a crack in the boards that she could make out a homemade bed bearing a lumpy moss mattress. In the corner was a chair with the back missing.

Going to the window, she pushed with all her might, but not one of the boards would give. Even if she could have broken free, Cordelia realized she would not know what direction to run. Pots rattled in the other room as someone began the evening meal. Outside her door the talk became louder, with all the men gathering to relax and wait for their supper. Someone must have brought a deck of cards, for she soon heard them calling their bets.

Fearing spiders, Cordelia cautiously sank down on the edge of the bed. Tears filled her eyes and spilled down her cheeks. What fate lay ahead of her she did not know, but somehow she must keep her wits about her if she wanted to survive. She cradled her face in her hands.

Poor Jack. He would be helpless when they came for him and Hettie. What could he do against so many? Jack might get off one shot, maybe two, but in his weakened condition the struggle would be short. Sitting there in the dark, Cordelia began to understand something of what he had been trying to tell her. How foolish of her to have taken his warning so lightly!

Her thoughts went to her brother. He would not learn of her disappearance for a while unless her captors used her as an incentive to break him. Were they all pawns in a much larger plan?

Crude remarks from the other room caused her face to burn, and she heard footsteps approach the door. Feeling around for a weapon to protect herself, Cordelia's heart pounded loudly, and she held her breath, staring at the narrow band of light under the door. The footsteps stopped, and she could hear someone breathing heavily on the other side. Were they listening to see if she was there? She made a slight noise with her foot and heard a muffled grunt. Whoever it was went away.

"All right, ya card sharks, are ya gonna eat these vittles, 'r do I th'ow 'em out?" a voice complained over the noise. Chairs scraped the floor, and the room grew quiet as the men got down to the serious business of eating.

"What about the woman?" someone asked.

"Fix 'er a plate, 'n' I'll fetch it to 'er," the leader replied; "'n' don't give 'er no knife 'r fork—jest a spoon."

A heavy tread announced his coming, and the key turned in the lock. The open door cast a shaft of light into the room.

"Here's some grub fer ya." Cordelia accepted the tin plate and cup thrust at her; then she was left in the dark. Common sense told her she needed to eat; besides, she hadn't eaten since morning, and the smell of food appealed to her empty stomach.

Pulling the chair over with her foot, she set the hot plate and cup on it and proceeded to eat the side meat, beans, and skillet-fried biscuit. The coffee was strong but good, and the hot drink lifted her spirits somewhat.

The hungry men outside her door made quick work of their food, for in a matter of minutes someone called for another game of cards.

"Not 'fore these utensils are cleaned up," growled one. "I done th' cookin', 'n' I sure ain't gonna wash yer dishes."

A lot of swearing and grumbling ensued, but finally all settled down for a good-natured game of chance. Cordelia listened to their conversation, hoping to identify the men, but they were very careful not to refer to one another by name.

Huddled there in the dark, stuffy room, each moment seemed like eons. The narrow band of light under the door had a hypnotic effect, and she found herself staring at it until her eyes hurt.

Ponderous steps shook the building as someone stomped onto the wooden porch. Those in the room outside her door fell silent. Chairs scraped the floor, the light beneath her door went out, and Cordelia could hear the card players trooping out to join whoever it was. There was the low murmur of voices followed by the sound of horses moving out; then all grew quiet.

In spite of her misery, Cordelia dozed on and off, startled awake by noises in the woods outside. Once she thought she heard someone clear his throat. Had one of her captors remained behind?

*   *   *

Dim morning light was penetrating the crack between the boards over the window when she was jarred awake by voices outside the hideout. Saddles hit the porch as the horses were relieved of their burdens. Someone trounced in, and by the rattle of the stove she knew breakfast was soon to follow. She knocked on her door, and the footsteps moved her way.

"Waddya want?" a voice on the other side of the door asked.

"Please, I need to—to get out and—and walk a little," she pleaded.

He moved away, and she strained her ears to catch what was being said. In a matter of moments, she was instructed to put on the blindfold. When she had done so, the key turned in the lock, and she was led outside.

"Please," Cordelia entreated, "let me take off the blindfold. I give my word not to run away. I can't see to walk without falling."

There was a slight pause; then the hand on her arm was removed, and she was left alone. "Ya got five minutes," a voice called from inside the house.

Cordelia pulled the blindfold from her eyes to find herself in a small clearing, surrounded by a thick stand of pines mingled with vine-entangled live oak trees. The house where she was being held captive was a small two-room shack. Smoke was curling from the makeshift stove pipe protruding from a window.

Where she was Cordelia had no idea, as she sought a place of privacy. Had the long ride taken her farther out on James Island or away from it? She could not tell, but of one thing she was sure. To try to escape on her own would be futile unless she had a horse.

Coming back around the house, she made a mental note of the poled enclosure where the animals were kept. Loathing to return to the dark room any sooner than necessary, she lingered as long as possible, enjoying the cool morning air.

"Aw right! Stand where ya are, and put that blindfold back on." She was becoming familiar with the men's voices and recognized this as the leader. Cordelia did as she was told, waiting until he came to where she stood. Allowing herself to be led back into the cabin, she found the blindfold was loose enough for her to see the large bony hand grasping her arm. A jagged scar ran diagonally across the top, starting just below the forefinger.

Except for the sound of meat frying, the room remained silent as Cordelia was moved through. The door had scarcely closed when she tore the blindfold from her face, and immediately her eyes sought out the pinpoint of light from the crack in the boards.

At least she could identify one of her captors, Cordelia thought triumphantly, resuming her seat on the bed. If there was just some way she could see into the other room, perhaps she could identify others. Leaning forward, she checked the keyhole to find "Scar-hand" had removed the key and she could see into the outer room. No one was in view at the moment, but she could make out the table. Her heart was beating fast as she straightened up. The time when they were eating would be her best chance.

When the call came for breakfast, it was a weary, subdued group who gathered. From where she sat, Cordelia could see several of the men. Two were facing her, and one sat with his back to her, hiding another on the other side. Of the two she could see clearly, one appeared young, with a boyish countenance that boasted a grubby, full, blond beard. As she watched, he removed his hat, tossing it to the floor behind him, running his fingers through a shock of unruly sandy hair. His cold, calculating eyes shocked her as he stared at her door.

Searching her mind, she could not remember seeing him around town. Turning her attention to the man beside him, she studied his dark visage, partially hidden by the black hat he wore.

"Hurry up with thet coffee!" he growled. "It's been a long night." Cordelia recognized the voice and strained to see him better. What she could see of his face was familiar to her, but where had she seen him before? With a slight intake of breath, she remembered the man who pushed in beside Baxter Spriggs the day they invaded her home.

"Who's gonna feed the girl?" the cook asked, moving among them to pour coffee.

"She can wait 'til I'm finished," scowled the leader, exposing the jagged scar on his hand as he raised the steaming cup to his lips.

Plates of food were passed down the table, and each turned his attention to filling his hungry stomach. As near as she could tell, there were five or six of them. When each finished, he picked up his cup and filed out to the porch. But "Scar-hand" remained seated. The cook set another plate on the table and ate his food.

Cordelia withdrew from the keyhole as the leader picked up her plate and got to his feet. "Put yer blindfold on in there!" he yelled, starting for her door. "Are ya ready?"

"Yes," she replied, pulling the piece of cloth over her eyes.

He unlocked the door and pushed the plate against her hand. "How long are you going to continue this outrage?" she demanded, anger rising within her. "Even a dog gets better treatment than this. The least you could do is give me water to drink and let me wash my hands."

"This ain't no picnic fer us either, lady," he snarled, "so stop yer whining. It'll all be over purty soon, 'n' ya won't have no more worries."

His meaning was not lost on her. As the key turned once again in the lock, she sank down on the bed, setting the plate aside untouched. Despair returned to haunt her, and she bowed before its onslaught. Tears filled her eyes, and she began to tremble uncontrollably. Why hadn't she listened to Jack? It was no one's fault but her own that she was in this predicament.

Her thoughts went to her friend Esther. Until she had married that wicked Tom Searles, she and Esther had gone to church together. Esther had always said God would make a way when we could not see our own. All one had to do was ask. Was that the reason Esther always seemed at peace? Did she dare ask God for help?

"Please, God, help me—I have no one to turn to," she whispered. "Send someone to help me. Give me the courage to face what is ahead. If my life is taken, I want to be ready to meet You. I'm so afraid, and I don't know what has happened to Hettie and Jack and my brother. Lord, we all need You so."

Cordelia sensed a comforting presence invade the dark, stuffy room, bringing peaceful calm over her. Raising her head heavenward, she felt a rush of joy fill her heart.

"Thank You, Father, for accepting me as Your child. I will trust You not only for myself but for Jack and Hettie and my brother. Only You can stop the evil in our land."

For a long while Cordelia sat there filled with wonder. Outside her door there was no sound except for the snores of tired men. Leaning against the wall, she felt her own eyes grow heavy with sleep.

11

JACK FELT A HAND on his shoulder, and he opened his eyes to see Mose leaning over him. Behind him stood Crawfish, holding a lamp in his hand, his face a study of concern.

"Cap'n, yo' been asleep fer a long time. Crawfish here wuz a worryin' 'bout yo'. Is yo' a' right?"

Jack looked from one worried face to the other, as memory of his narrow escape came back to him.

"Hettie?"

"Don' know, Cap'n. Ever'body been too scared t' go!"

"How long have I been here?"

"Crawfish brung yo' las' night, Cap'n," Mose answered.

"What time is it?"

"It be almost midnight, Cap'n."

Jack raised himself up on his elbows. The soreness in his chest was almost gone. Mose stepped back as he swung his legs off the bed.

"Got anything to eat?"

Mose nodded and left the room.

"Crawfish, where's Prince?"

"He's over t' my place, Cap'n, 'n' he's doin' jest fine."

There was a knock at the door, and when Mose went to see about it, Jack heard a woman's voice say, "Is dat Crawfish o'er here?"

"Who's wantin' t' know?" Mose queried.

"I be his sister 'n' dis be my boy," the woman answered. "We live out a ways." Noting Mose's hesitation, her voice took on an urgent tone. "My boy know somethin' y'all oughter know."

Mose stood back, allowing her to enter. "Wait here," he said, returning to where Crawfish and Jack had paused to listen.

Crawfish nodded at Mose, and he motioned her into the room, closing the door. The woman eyed Jack suspiciously, but Crawfish spoke up on his behalf.

"Cap'n's a friend. Say wha'cha come fer."

She prodded the wide-eyed, grown boy at her side. "G'won—tell Crawfish wha' yo' seen out on James Island."

The young man blinked. "I wuz out dat away huntin' yestiddy aft'noon, 'n' I seen dis fine buggy comin' 'long de road," he began. "De folks didn't see me, 'cause I wuz standin' by a big ol' oak. Den dese men rode outta de woods. Dey wuz all wearin' somethin' over dere faces. I thinks t' myself, Somethin's gonna hap'n."

His words spilled over one another as he related what he had seen. When he reached the point at which the woman was dragged from the carriage, Jack leaped to his feet, wild-eyed and shaking. Grabbing the startled young man by the arm, he cried, "What did she look like?"

"She wuz real purty, 'n'—'n' she wuz wit dat fella what works at de bank.".

"Cordelia." Jack's knees buckled beneath him, and he sank down onto the bed. Crenshaw had sacrificed Cordelia in order to ruin her brother. She would be allowed to live only until their terrible plan succeeded. His mind raced as he thought of her being in their hands for more than 24 hours. He dare not think of what atrocities she might be suffering.

"What's your name, son?" Jack asked.

"Toby."

"Toby, can you take me there?"

"Yes suh, but beggin' yo' pardon, suh—it ain't safe fer a Toby t' be seen pokin' 'roun' dere."

"I know, Toby, but if you'll give me the directions—Crawfish, will you saddle Prince for me?"

"Cap'n, ya cain't go ridin' off in the night!" Crawfish argued, his genial face wrinkled with anxiety. "That's when them nightriders be out. Ya best wait 'til mornin' when they creeps back int' their holes."

Jack hesitated, knowing the old man was right. "But Cordelia's out there in the hands of those cutthroats." His voice broke. "God only knows what she's going through."

Crawfish laid a big hand on Jack's shoulder, "You's right, Cap'n," he said solemnly. "God do know what she's goin' through. I believes she's gonna be all right. Ain't that so, Mose?"

"Sho' nuff, Cap'n," Mose agreed wholeheartedly. "Yo' just waits 'til mornin' 'n' take a ride out dat away. What yo' needs now is somethin' t' eat—den we'll talk."

Collard greens cooked with salt pork, corn pone, and boiled potatoes were brought to Jack, and he ate heartily as the others gathered in the other room. While he ate, Jack noticed his saddlebags lying on a box in the corner. If Mose's wife had a pair of scissors, he'd get rid of his beard, he decided. Then with some borrowed clothes, perhaps his appearance could be altered enough that the enemy might not recognize him. Satisfied with this train of thought, Jack laid his plate aside.

"Cap'n, we been talkin', 'n' we come up with a plan," Mose spoke up. "Dere's 'n old black buryin' ground out dat way, back in a field nearby dem woods. We've decided t' have us a fun'ral tomorrow."

For the next hour they laid careful plans. When all were satisfied they had thought of every detail, the group dispersed to take care of their assignments. Word was to be passed along to draw a good-sized crowd.

Jack returned to his bed to rest and wait, but sleep evaded him. Tortured by thoughts of what Cordelia might be going through, he tossed and turned as his imagination ran wild. He assailed himself bitterly for her plight. Had he not been so caught up in his own act of revenge, he would have seen the dangerous position she had placed herself in by harboring him.

Lying there, he kept seeing her pleading eyes, filled with tears, before him. Anguish rolled over him like ocean waves. Suddenly realizing how empty his life would be without her, Jack vowed to go save her at all costs. The rough-hewn walls of the room seemed to close in on him, and he slipped outside to escape the stifling heat.

Sitting there on the step, he found little comfort in the beauty of the starlit night. Off in the trees a hoot owl gave its eerie cry. Many nights out on the battlefield he had heard that sound mingled with the cries of wounded men, many who saw it as an omen.

Jack was glad when it faded in the distance. Looking up at the stars, he was reminded of the many evenings he had spent as a lad listening to the sounds of the night while his father talked of the Lord's goodness. Often the freed slaves would gather to sit on the ground to hear what he had to say, singing their spirituals.

Jack bowed his head, recalling the cadence of his father's voice as it would rise and fall when he quoted the Scriptures. What was the one he had so often talked about? Was it the first psalm?

He searched his mind to remember how it started. It was something about walking, standing, and sitting with sinners. He shook his head at the memory of the day he had come home proudly wearing his first gun and holster. From that moment on, the relationship between him and his father deteriorated. Later Jack's father told him in no uncertain terms that no son of his would wear a gun in his house. Until he left to fight in the war, Jack had honored his father's request, defiantly strapping on his gun the day he walked away forever.

Now looking back, Jack regretted the action that had brought so much sorrow to his father's heart. Where had he gone wrong? Like David of old, he had become a warrior with blood on his hands. Was there any hope or help for him?

Just before Jack had left home, his father had dwelt night after night on the first psalm, tying it to 1 John 1:9. He could still remember the verse: "If we confess our sins, he is faithful and just to forgive us our sins, and to cleanse us from all unrighteousness." Jack had known it was for his benefit and resented the effort, often walking away.

Jack stared into the night, searching his heart. The old feeling of resentment was gone, and, looking back, Jack realized it was a father's love for his wayward son that prompted his persistence. Tears came to his eyes. Jack had been invincible—that is, until a bullet in the dark nearly snuffed out his life. His hand went to the scar he would carry the rest of his life. That, and the love of Cordelia Dureen, had drawn him to the realization of how precious life could really be.

Dawn was breaking in the east when he made his decision. "Forgive me, Lord. I have spurned everyone who has tried to help me, even this woman You've sent to love me and care for me. Help me return to the faith of my father. I pray not for myself only, but for Cordelia. Please, God—stay with her and keep her safe, and also these people who are risking their lives to help me. If it is Your will that I live, I will teach my household Your Word."

Jack heard a quiet step behind him, and Mose sat down, wiping the sleepiness from his eyes with his fingers.

"Yo' been out here all night?"

"Mostly," Jack replied, raising his head to look at his companion with bloodshot eyes.

Mose shook his head. "Thinkin' 'bout her?"

"Yes, I hate every moment she'll have to spend in their evil hands, but I realized last night that God has a purpose in all things. I've got to believe that or lose my mind." Jack's voice grew thick.

"Dat's good, Cap'n," Mose responded, squeezing his shoulder. The old man cast an appraising glance at the sky. "Gonna be a nice day for de fun'ral—hot, tho'. Ain't a leaf stirrin'. Hope one of dem storms ain't a brewin'. Last one pushed water clean up de river, 'n' dere was water runnin' a foot deep in de yard. Minners were swimmin' right by de porch here. The wind sound like a woman screamin'. Nearly took de roof off. Blew Crawfish's barn roof off, sho' nuff!"

"Mose, I learned a long time ago you can't do anything about the weather except endure it," Jack said, chuckling at Mose's narration.

"Reckon so, Cap'n," Mose responded, getting to his feet. "Come on in—smells like somethin's on de table."

*   *   *

Many people along the dusty street stopped to gaze at the strange procession making its way toward the river. Along the way others joined the group, riding their mules. Some climbed on other mule-drawn wagons to follow behind the wagon bearing a wooden box, and what appeared to be the grieving widow and her children. All were dressed in their very best "fun'ral" clothes.

Waiting for the ferry, the men gathered in a tight knot around the wagon bearing the coffin, talking in low tones. Crawfish watched as the ferry with several riders and their horses made its way toward them. One of the riders he recognized as Baxter Spriggs.

"Everybody hold steady—riders comin'," he warned. "Act natural."

The whispered warning went through the group like wildfire. Some broke out into a song, while others stared nervously at the ferry putting in to shore.

Spriggs stared at the sight with more than a casual curiosity as "Swing Low, Sweet Chariot" floated out on the morning air.

"Now what are those people up to?" he growled.

"Looks like a funeral to me, boss," one of the riders spoke up.

"I'd like to bury the whole lot of 'em," Spriggs answered darkly, taking his time to disembark. "Let 'em wait."

Once on shore, the riders paused with their horses for a smoke, blocking the entrance to the boat until it left for the other shore. Then they slowly rode away, laughing among themselves.

Forced to wait in the heat, the funeral entourage sought relief in the shade of some trees nearby. It took nearly an hour for them to get across the river, where others waited in subdued anger to join them. Among them was Jess, who rode his horse close to the wagon.

"Crawfish, I's reckonin' dis be de onlyest fun'ral I ever been at where de dead's gonna rise agin," he said softly.

"Mornin', Jess. Ya'll be lookin' better. How's Mantie?"

"Toler'ble, Crawfish, jest toler'ble," Jess answered. "She be some happier now days."

Once beyond the turnoff to James Island, the group made better progress. When they got to the point where the outlaw trail branched off in the woods, Crawfish's nephew, with an air of importance, pointed to where the kidnapping took place.

One of the women in the wagon spotted Cordelia's hat, and Jess rode over to retrieve it. Deeper and deeper into the dense woods they went, grateful at least for the shade. Conversation dwindled as one after the other fell into watchful silence. When they came to another fork in the road, Toby appeared from the trees to point to the left across a long field. "De burying ground's o'er dere. See de gate leadin' in? Dere's an ol' shack up 'atta way, back in de trees offen t' the right," he said.

Crawfish took a large white handkerchief from his pocket to wipe the perspiration from his brow. "Wadda ya think, Mose?"

"It be time," Mose responded in a quiet, steady voice from where he sat in the back with the casket. Whispering among themselves, the women sat fanning and mopping their faces as apprehension mounted.

"Aw' right, ever'body—jest hold steady," Crawfish said. "Ya women hep Mose wi' that lid back yonder. Jess, you 'n' de dead best get goin'. We'll cover fer ya'll. Give de cap'n yer hoss, 'n' yo' take Mose's."

Jack was glad to see the light of day again. It had been all he could do to lie in that box so long.

"Keep their attention, Mose," he whispered, slipping to the ground, "and everybody pray a lot." With a wave of his hand he stepped into the saddle and rode off with Jess and Toby.

Toby took the lead for a short way, then stopped and slid from the saddle. Jack and Jess followed suit. Without speaking, Toby motioned them to his side. Ahead was an old homestead that showed signs of some recent repair. Jack guessed the room to the side with the boarded-up window would be where Cordelia was being held.

The murmur of men's voices drifted to them through the quiet of the giant oak trees. From where he stood, Toby spotted a wild razorback hog rooting for acorns.

"Jist my luck, t' see 'im when I can't shoot my gun," he complained in a whisper to Jess.

"How many men's in there?" Jack asked, nudging Toby with his elbow.

"Don't reckon I know fer sure now, but dey wuz 'bout ha'f dozen last time I seen," Toby answered.

"Check your guns, men," Jack admonished. Off in the distance the funeral procession began to sing. "The party's about to begin," Jack said. He pulled his revolver and checked the chamber.

In a matter of minutes, someone from in the shack shouted, "What's goin' on out there?"

"Looks like a bunch of blacks headin' fer that old graveyard," the man on the porch shouted back. "Come out here!"

The shack was built up off the ground, as was the custom, and from where they crouched, Jack, Toby, and Jess could see two sets of legs appear as men slid off the porch.

"There's two of them," Jack whispered. "Now if more of them would only step out, it'd be easier."

Soon others joined the two, and Jack made the decision to move in. "Tie those rags over your faces, and pull your hats low," he said, doing the same. "They're not the only ones who can play that game. Jess, you come up this side; Toby and I will slip around on the right. When I make my move, you two back me up."

"We're with ya, Cap'n," Jess spoke up.

In a matter of seconds, Jack peered around the corner of the building to see six men standing in the yard with their backs to him, looking intently across the field.

"Couple of ya oughter ride over 'n' see what it's all about," the apparent leader advised.

None turned quick enough to see the tall figure step out behind them until it was too late. "Don't anyone move," Jack warned, his voice deadly cold, "or we just may have more'n one funeral on our hands. Hands away from your guns and in the air."

The men stiffened, hands reaching toward their sides. The large man spun around to face Jack, his eyes darting back and forth for an avenue of escape.

"I wouldn't make any wrong moves if I were you," Jack warned, reading his intent. "There's a man behind you who's just itching for some target practice with that new rifle of his. Now take it nice and easy. You on the left—unload your holster and drop it back of you. The rest of you do the same."

The man hesitated, looking at the big man who was the obvious leader. Jack fired a well-aimed shot that kicked up the dirt at the man's foot. He jumped, then hurried to comply.

"All right, boys, you can move in now—I think these gents just got my message, but keep your eyes on them," Jack called to Jess and Toby when all had dropped their weapons.

Disarmed and hog-tied with their own ropes, the glaring, cursing men were left in the charge of Jess and Toby while Jack went in search of Cordelia. He approached the house with care, glancing through the window. The first room appeared to be empty.

"That girl won't want t' see the likes of him after we got done with her, will she, boys?" the big man with a scar on his hand flung after Jack tauntingly.

Jess walked over and stuck his rifle hard against the man's head. There was no need for him to say a word, for the man's jaw snapped shut and his face blanched.

Jack entered the hideout to cross noiselessly toward the door leading into the other room, staying out of line of a bullet that might come unexpectedly. A man can make an easy target standing in front of a door when he doesn't know what's on the other side. He paused, listening for the slightest sound. With his left hand he reached out to turn the knob. The door was locked.

"Cordelia," he called softly.

He heard a glad cry, then the sound of footsteps. "Jack! Is that you?"

"Yes. Are you alone?"

"Yes."

"Open the door."

"I can't. The man with the scar on his hand has the key in his vest pocket."

Jack retrieved the key, and when the door swung open, Cordelia collapsed into his arms.

"Jack, I heard the singing, then the shot—and—oh Jack, I could only hope—," she sobbed into his chest.

"Cordelia—dearest, I'm here—you're safe now." Jack felt her trembling and found himself kissing her hair over and over again. He remembered the danger they were in and pushed her away abruptly. "Hurry now—others may ride in," he finally managed to say. Quickly he led her out into the light.

"Put blindfolds on those men, and put them on their horses; tie a rope from one neck to the other, just in case one of them gets any idea of making a break for it," Jack instructed Jess and Toby, who silently obeyed.

Toby brought their horses in, and Jack took Jess's mount, leaning to take Cordelia in his arms when Jess handed her up to him. Lying with her head on his shoulder, Cordelia stared mutely at Jack's smooth-shaven face. He led off at a fast trot to where Crawfish, Mose, and the others waited. No one spoke as the kidnappers were loaded into Crawfish's big wagon and covered with a tarp.

"This ain't human," one of them complained. "We'll suffocate in this heat!"

"Quit your snivelin'," snarled the leader.

"There's men riding shotgun back there with you," Jack warned. "First one to speak up will wish he hadn't."

They were off, the wagon bumping over the rough road. Everyone kept quiet until the group reached the parting of the ways. Mose took charge of the group going across the river to Charleston, and Crawfish went with Jack, Toby, and Jess on the long ride to George Medford's place. There Cordelia was given into Mrs. Medford's capable hands for some much-needed rest, and the prisoners were placed under guard in a strong building.

Jack filled Medford in on what had happened since they had last met. Medford sat in disbelief, listening intently to Jack's story. "These are terrible times, Captain," he said, shaking his head sadly. "These must be desperate men."

"Not desperate, George," Jack corrected, "just greedy for power and money. They look on the big plantation owners as folks who are there for the picking. Our only hope is to organize the big planters to rise up against the encroachers."

"Do ya think we can do that?" Medford asked hopefully.

"I think I hold the trump card now. None of these men will take what happened to Cordelia Dureen lightly. But we must act at once. Get word to John Dreyton that I've been shot and am asking for him. He'll come. When he sees and hears what's taken place, it will stir him to action. John is the key in persuading the other planters to join us."

"I think you're right," said Medford. "I'll ride over immediately. Meanwhile, you look like some rest would do ya some good. There's a room down at the end of the hall with a good bed. Help yourself." Medford got to his feet. "By the way, I see you've shaved off the beard."

"Uh huh," Jack responded, "I'd never worn one before—always hated them. Just grew it as a disguise. I reckoned since the cat was out of the bag, I didn't need it now."

Medford nodded his response, picked up his hat, and left. Jack sought the comfort of the room Medford had suggested, stretching out wearily on the bed. Except for a small ache in the area of his wound, he felt amazingly well after the ordeal of this day.

Over his head, he could hear the murmur of a woman's voice, and his thoughts returned to the brief time he had held Cordelia in his arms there at the shack. He had resisted the urge to declare his love to her—there would be time for that, he hoped.

One thing troubled him, however: had Cordelia heard the coarse remarks of the bandit leader? It would be amiss to think she hadn't. How could she have helped but hear, with such thin walls? His heart went out to her, for certainly she would feel even more violated. She would need to have a lot of love and understanding to overcome her horrible experience. When this was over, he would take her away.

≡ *12* ≡

JACK AWAKENED to someone shaking his shoulder. He opened his eyes to see George Medford standing over him.

"Captain Brevard, John's here t' see you. He's waitin' in the parlor."

"Tell him I'll be there in a moment," Jack responded, pushing himself up on the side of the bed. After Medford had gone, Jack availed himself of the water and clean towels on the washstand. The water was refreshing, and soon he felt presentable.

"Ah—here he is," Medford exclaimed when he put in his appearance. "You're lookin' better."

John Dreyton stood to his feet to greet him. "Jack, I was sorry to hear about what happened, but it's good to see you lookin' so well, considerin' what you've gone through."

"Evening, John—I'm glad you've come," Jack responded. "The last time we were together, you told me to let you know if I needed anything. I'm not asking necessarily for myself, but for Medford and Cordelia and all the people who are being threatened, hurt, and destroyed."

"Have a seat, gentlemen, and I'll see about havin' some coffee brought in," their host said, leaving the room.

"Tell me about your accident," Dreyton urged as he lowered himself, spreading his tall, well-dressed form into the overstuffed chair. His gray eyes were friendly.

Jack pulled a chair over closer where he could see Dreyton's face clearly in the light. "It wasn't an accident, John. Someone was laying for me outside the inn. If it hadn't been

153

for old Doc Steen and Cordelia, I wouldn't be here to tell you the story."

Medford returned, closed the door behind him, and sat down. Jack related the events leading up to Cordelia's capture, watching disbelief turn to anger and outrage when he got to the part about Wilford Crenshaw's betrayal of her.

"Where is she now?" Dreyton asked gravely.

"I'm coming to that," Jack answered with great emotion.

Mantie came in with a tray, and he waited until she had gone before going on to relate the rest of the details. "I brought Cordelia here, where I knew she'd be safe; I haven't seen her since," Jack concluded.

Dreyton slammed his fist down on the arm of his chair. "What a dastardly deed! I thought Crenshaw practically worshiped Cordelia!"

"He loves money and power more," Jack said. "No doubt he was promised she wouldn't be hurt and that he could rescue her, making a great impression so that she would marry him. Who knows? There's a mastermind behind all of this, John, and I'm convinced he'll let nothing stand in his way to achieve his goals. I believe even you big plantation owners are targeted for ruin once he's rid of the people like Medford here. Whoever it is thinks you planters are a bunch of party-givers and will be easy pushovers. Crenshaw probably keeps him informed on what each of you owe to the bank. I don't know how many are in their gang, but we've cut down their number by six."

"Where are these men?"

"We have them here under guard. We need help in finding an honest lawman we can turn them over to. Perhaps you can handle that end of it." Jack paused, waiting for Dreyton's response.

"I can. The governor is a friend of mine. I'll get word to him right away about what's goin' on down here. He knows Cordelia Dureen well and will be greatly disturbed at her treatment. What we need is a U.S. marshall to back us in case

Sheriff Duganne is mixed up in all this. Do you have any suspicion he is?"

"No. I really don't know the man. But the fact he didn't even investigate my shooting or the beatings leads me to suspect he's conveniently looking the other way."

"You may be right," Dreyton agreed. "Doesn't make sense he didn't even ask questions."

"How well do you know Otis J. Teasberry?" Jack asked suddenly.

"Not very well," Dreyton answered candidly. "He's been in the area only a short while. Seems a likable chap. He's been to the house once or twice. As a matter of fact, Crenshaw brought him along. Martha has found him to be an excellent dancer. That seems to go a long way with these women." He laughed.

"He's one of them," Jack announced without humor.

"You don't say?" Dreyton responded in surprise. His gray eyes grew deadly serious. "Are you sure?"

"Positive," Jack stated emphatically.

"Well, wadda ya know?" Medford interjected, breaking his silence. "He'd be the one who'd handle the legal side of it for 'em."

"John, can you organize a secret meeting of the big plantation owners? Medford here says he can get a few of the smaller landowners. The sooner the better. Depending on their activities, Baxter Spriggs and his men will discover what we did today, and things will start happening. If you can get the word around, tell the planters to be prepared for what seems to be innocent visits. It'd be wise to arm yourselves so you don't get caught off guard."

"Most of us have lately taken to carryin' a weapon," Dreyton assured him, flipping his coat open to reveal the gun at his side. His eyes became troubled. "Will Cordelia be all right?"

"I think so, John. She's with Mrs. Medford."

"May I see her?"

"I'll see," Medford offered, leaving the room.

While they waited, Jack and Dreyton made plans for the meeting. It would be held at Dreyton Hall after they had heard from the governor.

Both men got to their feet expectantly at Medford's return. "The lass doesn't want t' see anyone," he informed them. "Wife says she cries a lot." Jack felt as if someone had punched him in the stomach. What had those men done to her?

"Poor dear!" Dreyton exclaimed, his handsome face a picture of distress. "Perhaps Martha can help. I know she'll want to come."

Picking up his hat, Dreyton walked to the door where he paused, "I'll do what I can, Jack. You can count on that." Turning to Medford, he asked, "How're you fixed on men, George?"

"I have two good ones—Jess 'n' Toby."

"I'll send a couple of my men over to help with the chores," Dreyton promised, taking his leave.

"'Preciate it, John!" Medford called after him.

*   *   *

More than a week had passed since Jack's talk with John Dreyton. Standing on the small porch off the kitchen, Jack spotted Jess, arms filled with empty plates, coming from the building where the prisoners were held. A broad smile broke across the young man's face when he looked up to see Jack watching him.

"Hey, Cap'n," he hailed. "I see yer up 'n' 'bout early dis mornin'. Ya even beat de sun up. Good thing, 'cause it's gonna be a hot one."

Jack waited until Jess came to the edge of the porch before speaking. "How are the prisoners faring?"

"Dey's all gettin' meaner 'n a bag full of snakes, Cap'n."

"Well, maybe that'll change soon, Jess. We're expecting a U.S. marshall to come anytime to take over. There's going to be a meeting of the planters at Dreyton Hall day after tomorrow. While we're gone, Jess, I want you and the others to stand guard around the place—do you understand? It isn't likely they'll move on us in the daytime, but you never know—we're pretty far out."

"Yes suh, Cap'n. We'll keep both eyes peeled."

"How's it working out with those men Dreyton sent over?"

"Oh, it be jest fine, Cap'n."

"Good! You ever been in love, Jess?"

"Yes suh," Jess answered with a wide, happy grin. "Ya know dat gran'darter o' Crawfish's? I 'tend to make 'er my woman."

Jack nodded. "Jess, upstairs is Mrs. Dureen. I'm counting on you to see nothing happens to her while I'm gone."

"Yes suh, Cap'n. You kin count on me."

After Jess had gone on into the kitchen with his load, Jack sat on the upper step thinking. He had not seen Cordelia since the day he had brought her here. She had allowed only Medford's wife and Mantie to see her. At first he had thought it was because of the terrible ordeal she had been through, but now it baffled him.

"There's a couple of men ridin' in," Medford announced quietly from the doorway, breaking into his reverie.

Jack joined Medford in the front yard to wait for their arrival. John Dreyton was one of them, and the other looked familiar to Jack. Only when they had drawn closer did Jack realize who it was. "Stanton Mulholland!" he exclaimed under his breath.

"Do ya know that man with Dreyton?" Medford asked without removing his eyes from the approaching riders.

"Sure do, George—we fought in the war together. Hailed from the mountains of Tennessee. He was one of the toughest and squarest men in our regiment."

Riding into the yard, the men dismounted to walk toward them, leading their horses.

"Mornin'—," Dreyton began but was drowned out by a whoop from his companion.

"Andrew Jackson Brevard, is that really you? Good heavens, man! I never thought I'd lay eyes on you again in this world. So ya *did* make it through prison!"

Jack's heart was full as he took hold of the big hand extended to him. "Howdy, Stant! It's sure good to see you again. What brings you into these parts?"

"I'm the U.S. marshall Mr. Dreyton sent for. I heard ya've been havin' some troubles down this a way."

"No use us all standin' here—come on in," Medford broke in, leading the way. "Mantie's rustlin' up some breakfast."

Seated around the table, the men appeased their appetites, reminiscing over the past. Jack finished first, pushing back his plate. Mantie came to refill the cups, and he sipped coffee while he waited for the rest.

"Bring your cups on in here," Medford suggested, heading for the parlor. After they were all in, he followed, closing the door.

"Jack, I haven't told the marshall here your story. I thought it best if you'd tell him the details yourself."

Jack paused until Medford drew up a chair, then began with his trip into the area this time, leaving out the reason for his coming. Marshall Mulholland listened with interest, inserting a question now and then. When Jack had finished, Mulholland sat with knitted, heavy brows, staring at him with thoughtful, clear-blue eyes. His large barrel-chested frame looked even larger in the small chair that bore his heavy weight.

"So Tom Searles is in this mix? I ain't surprised," he commented at length.

Jack accepted his comment without reply. It had been a well-known fact in the regiment that Searles and Mulholland did not get along with each other.

"Well, I'm glad ya've made it through the gunshot, Jack. I've taken on a few myself. It ain't much fun. What are your plans from here?" Mulholland spread his large hands on his knees.

"Other than turning these men over to you for safekeeping, we've set a meeting with the planters in the area. John here can tell you the details on that."

"Are ya sure that's all ya have on your mind?" Marshall Mulholland queried, his eyes boring into Jack's.

Without asking, Jack knew Dreyton had told Mulholland he was on the prowl for Clemson.

"It is at the moment," he replied coolly, an easy smile breaking across his face.

Mulholland was not fooled by the outward demeanor but declined to make further comment. He would see to it later.

"Good! Now let's take a look at them pris'ners. By the way, I understand Cordelia Dureen is here. Would someone tell her I'd like t' ask her a few questions?" He rose from his chair to give a hitch to his trousers.

"I'll take care of it, George, if you'll show Marshall Mulholland where the men are being held," Jack spoke up quickly.

Medford gave Jack a peculiar glance but complied with his wishes. Jack did not stop to analyze its meaning but headed for the stairs. Glancing toward the kitchen, he saw Mrs. Medford talking to Mantie. He was relieved to know Cordelia would be in her room alone. Quietly taking the steps two at a time, he paused briefly before the door, which was slightly ajar. From where he stood he could see Cordelia sitting with her back to him. Jack pushed the door open, and it made a sound.

Laying aside the book she was reading, Cordelia rose from her chair. "Oh, is breakfast—?" she said, expecting it to be Mrs. Medford or Mantie. But when she turned to see Jack standing there, her face paled, and she stiffened noticeably.

"U.S. Marshall Stanton Mulholland is downstairs and wants to speak to you; I—I said I would tell you," he explained, shocked at the dark circles under her eyes and the pallor of her face.

"Thank you, Captain Brevard—tell the marshall I shall be ready," she said tersely, taking her seat. Picking up her book, she pretended to ignore his presence.

"Cordelia—I wanted to—I needed to see you," he stammered, not knowing where to start. When she did not respond, Jack came forward to kneel before her. There were tears in her eyes.

"Cordelia, look at me," he pleaded. "I've been so worried! What's wrong—why have you been avoiding me? I've wanted so much to tell you what's happened to me—how much I love you.

"When Toby told what Crenshaw and those men did to you, I nearly went out of my mind. I wanted to ride out on Prince and rescue you right away, but Crawfish and Mose knew how foolish one against so many would be. They made me see their plan and offered to help." He tilted her chin up. "Listen to me, dear. I love you, and I don't want to face a life without you by my side. I thought I had lost you and prayed God would give you back to me. When all this is over, will you marry me?"

"You heard what that horrible man said about me," she whispered, tears rolling down her cheeks. "I thought you believed him when you pushed me away there at the cabin. I've been so ashamed."

"Ahh! So that's it!" Jack breathed, his troubled face brightening somewhat. "Cordelia, when I saw you there, all I wanted to do was hold you in my arms and never let you go," Jack assured her, taking her trembling hands in his, "but I knew I must hurry to get you and everyone else out of there before others rode in on us. A lot of good people would have been hurt, even killed."

"It wouldn't have made any difference to you if they—if they—?" she asked, her voice failing her.

Raising her violet eyes to meet his, Cordelia was overwhelmed by the compassion she saw there. "I would have been deeply grieved for your sake," Jack answered honestly, returning her studied gaze, "but it would not have changed my love for you. Tell me what happened . . ."

Listening with mixed emotions as the story unfolded, Jack decided on a course of action when she tearfully concluded.

"Come with me—I want you to meet someone," Jack went on, helping her up.

He led her down the stairs and out into the yard to where Medford and Dreyton stood talking to the impressive-looking man with a star on his chest.

"Wait here," he said, leaving her a few feet away.

She watched as they talked, taking note of the sympathetic glances made in her direction. When Jack returned to her side, the man with the star on his chest came with him.

"Cordelia, this is Stant Mulholland, the U.S. marshall. He's a good friend of mine."

"Miz Dureen," Mulholland acknowledged with a broad smile. "Ma'am, I'm awful sorry 'bout all this. I'll only take a minute. It's meant for your good." Taking her by the arm, he led her into the storage room serving as a prison.

Before her sat the six men who had abducted her. It was the first time she had seen them all face-to-face. Each had his feet tied with a rope that extended to encircle his neck. Hands were tied behind his back.

"Now, Miz Dureen, I know this ain't easy for ya, but I want ya t' identify the men that so much as laid a hand on ya," Marshall Mulholland drawled in a kind voice.

The men all began to curse and swear at the big man bearing a scar on his hand. "See what yer dirty mouth's got us into?" one flung at him accusingly, cutting loose with a string of oaths.

"Shaddup, ya buncha yellow-livered skunks—yer just afraid to admit what ya did!" the big man sneered back at them.

"Watch your mouth!" Mulholland bellowed. "If we have t' gag ya, we will. Now, ma'am, go ahead."

Cordelia stared at each one until her eyes centered accusingly on the one she had come to call Scar-hand. Before she could speak, however, the youngest of the group spoke up loudly. "Marshall, honest, ain't none of us laid a finger on that woman 'ceptin' him." He spit at his leader. "He's the onlyest one what had a key."

Quick as a wink, Cordelia jerked Jack's big gun from its holster, pointing it at Scar-hand. "Tell them what you did to me!" she cried, the weapon wobbling in her hand as her finger felt for the trigger.

"I didn't lay a hand on ya 'ceptin' t' lead ya around!" the man shouted hoarsely, his eyes bulging in their sockets. "I only said what I did back there t' get even. Put thet gun down afore it goes off!"

"Haw! Haw! Look at our fearless leader now—he's afraid of a slip of a woman!" one of his cohorts yelled gleefully. "Now who's yeller?"

"Cordelia, be careful," Jack urged in a quiet, steady voice, reaching from behind her. "The gun has a hair trigger. Give it to me."

The gun went off with an earsplitting roar, splintering a board in the wall, barely missing the white-faced, terror-stricken man. Cordelia felt a sick feeling in the pit of her stomach, and she collapsed against Jack.

Recovering the revolver, Jack jammed it into his holster and turned Cordelia over to Dreyton, who led her out. Then Jack stepped close to the frightened man and with cold, blazing eyes fastened on his face, he said, "If you ever so much as whisper again what you said to me back at that shack, I'll hunt you down, and I won't miss." Abruptly he turned and walked out.

"Ya better listen t' him, fella—I've seen him in action," Mulholland advised coldly, then followed Jack out, locking the door behind them.

Medford led Cordelia back into the house, but Dreyton stood waiting for Jack and Mulholland. He had seen that look on Jack's face before and read what it meant. The man had gotten off easy.

"Dreyton, I reckon to stay over here for the night," Mulholland said. "These folks seem kinda shorthanded. Send my deputies over when ya get back. If anybody comes a callin' in the night, we'll have a surprise party for 'em."

"Well, looks like everything's under control here," Dreyton remarked. "Guess I better be gettin' back to Martha."

"John, I don't like to see you ride back alone; take those two men you sent over with you," Jack insisted. "With Stanton's deputies coming, we'll have plenty of help over here."

"Good idea, Dreyton," Mulholland chimed in. "One can't be careful enough."

Dreyton turned to Medford, who came from the house to join them. "How is she, George?"

"Like all our wives, she's a strong woman. She knowed what she was doin' 'n' feels vindicated afore witnesses."

"She'll make some lucky cuss a good wife," Mulholland spoke up in admiration. "That girl's got grit!"

Dreyton shot a quick glance at Jack. He and Martha had always had a liking for the man but knew nothing of his financial position. Impeccably dressed, he had always looked successful, and Martha had wondered why he had never settled down. If Cordelia was in love with him, she could do no better. He would turn the head of any woman, but a woman needed more—and certainly not a man bent on murder.

"Stant, when these crooks realize we're on to them, they're going to run like rats," Jack said thoughtfully, unaware of his friend's smug appraisal.

"The cap'n's right," Medford interrupted. "At least we got the goods on some of 'em. But how can we cut him out t' herd without raisin' suspicions 'n' spookin' the mastermind who's behind all this?"

"Maybe I have the solution," Dreyton spoke up. "Why don't I invite Crenshaw to the meetin' Saturday? I'll let him think it's purely a social thing."

"Good idea! What do you think, Stant?" Jack said, turning to Mulholland.

"Might work. I was plannin' t' be there anyways. I'm not hankerin' for a shootout if we can avoid sheddin' blood."

"Then I'll set the trap," Dreyton agreed, picking up the reins of his horse.

"Come on in the house, Marshall," Medford said as Dreyton vanished around the barn. "No use us standin' out here in the heat."

"When did you get in to Dreyton Hall, Stant?" Jack asked casually as Medford departed to the house to see about some cool drinks.

"We camped on the trail last night 'n' got in early this mornin'. Them boys of mine ain't gonna be in too good a mood lessen they get 'em some shut-eye. I sure hope nothin' breaks loose t'night, 'cause they'll be spoilin' for a fight. Why, they're the meanest-ridin'est bunch ya ever seen, Jack, 'n' they're worse when they get riled." Mulholland pulled his heavy weight up the steps.

"Did you know Sandy Ravenswood's running a ferry down on the Edisto?" Jack asked, sliding a rocker to the shady side of the veranda. "I spent the night there coming up."

"Ya don't say? How's ol' Sandy doin'?" Mulholland asked, lowering his heavy bulk into the seat Jack offered.

"He ended up losing that leg, you know. He's wearing a peg, but he gets around real good. Same old Sandy."

"Well, they ain't many what come through the war without takin' on some lead, except you 'n' a few others, Jack."

"In my case, Stant, 'takin' on some lead,' as you call it, would have been easier," Jack responded bitterly, hunkering down to lean against a post.

"Yeah, I heard what happened t' ya, Jack," Mulholland said, taking out a big red handkerchief to mop the perspiration from his brow. "But it's best t' put it behind ya now. John told me you was bent t' go gunnin' for the man who betrayed ya. I reckon it's my duty as U.S. marshall t' warn ya I'd have t' run ya in for murder."

From her room overhead, Cordelia lay listening to their conversation coming through her open window. She waited for Jack's reply, but none came. Medford returned to join them, and the subject was dropped. The drone of their voices soon lulled her to sleep.

≡ *13* ≡

MULHOLLAND'S DEPUTIES put in their appearance just in time to stow their gear and wash up for supper. Jack took an instant liking to all of them. Hank was the eldest, and it was easy to see the younger ones looked up to him. Broad of shoulder with a brawny build, he had a round, amiable face decorated with a heavy mustache. Alert and attentive, his clear blue eyes missed nothing.

Reddy was a bandy-legged, sinewy, red-headed, ruddy-faced fellow with a bent for telling jokes. His relaxed, careless demeanor didn't fool Jack, though, for his dark eyes were level and honest.

R. Q. was the quiet one. He sat aloof, satisfied to listen to the others, his face obscure in the shadows of the big hat he wore. His right hand always hovered near his gun, giving Jack the impression he was a steel trap set to go off.

"It's his Indian blood," Reddy teased. "We found him under a tepee that the wind blew over."

Jake appeared to be the youngest but wise beyond his years. Good manners bore evidence he had been the recipient of a caring family. His pleasant, boyish face was wreathed in smiles as he played with the several dogs gathered around the group on the porch. In some ways he reminded Jack of his brother who, he realized with a pang in his heart, would have been about this boy's age.

When supper was announced, Jack took note of the ease with which Hank and R. Q. slipped away in the dark. He had seen that kind of discipline in the colonel's men.

Supper was a cordial affair with Mrs. Medford, Mantie, and Cordelia serving them. Eating after the manner of hungry men, Reddy and Jake made quick work of their food and, without lingering, went to relieve the other men.

After the meal was over, little time was spent in further conversation and merriment. The weary men trooped off to seek their bedrolls. Only Jack lingered, hoping to have a moment with Cordelia, but she shyly eluded him, slipping to her room.

Unable to sleep, Jack stood in the shadows on the porch long after the house had grown silent and dark. Except during the years he had spent as a prisoner of war, he always liked this hour of the day the most. A slight breeze stirred in the drooping trees, bringing relief from the oppressive heat that had reigned all day.

Off to his right, a slight movement caught his ear. Jack pulled his revolver and waited, listening intently.

"I reckon I better let you know I'm here," a quiet voice came through the dark. "I heard you clear leather."

Jack recognized the voice as Reddy's and slipped his gun back into its sheath. Reddy moved noisily to his side with the comment "Awful quiet out here, ain't it? Kinda gives a body the creeps."

"Too quiet," Jack answered. "Who else is on watch?"

"That fella named Jess, and I reckon Hank is sleepin' with one eye open."

"Where'd they quarter?"

"Out in that little buildin' next to where the pris'ners are," Reddy drawled.

"Listen!" Jack whispered, holding up a hand.

There was a swooshing sound, then a single shot moved them into action. Out back, yells could be heard as sleepy men piled into the yard. Jack and Reddy raced around the house to find the barn afire, flames greedily eating at the hay stored there.

"Keep out of the light, men—they'll pick ya off from the dark!" roared Mulholland, who came running, fastening his gun belt as he came.

"Prince!" Jack shouted, starting to run, but Reddy caught his arm to restrain him.

"Hold on, Cap'n! Ya just can't go bargin' out there t' get yourself killed!"

"I can't stand by and let him burn to death either!" Jack tried frantically to tear himself away.

Before Jack could manage to free himself, there was a terrible crash, followed by the twang of bullets. Prince and the other horses plunged from the burning barn to run off in the dark, and the rest of the stock poured from the building behind them. Terrified calves bawled after their vanishing mothers, and hogs went squealing into the brush.

"Who was in the barn?" Jack yelled over the roar as the roof fell in with a crash.

"Last I seen, Jess was headed thataway!" Reddy shouted in his ear.

Jack turned away, sick to his stomach. There was no chance Jess would make it out of that inferno alive. Medford, rifle in hand, came running into the yard. His wife and Cordelia followed as far as the porch to watch in horror.

"Get back in the house!" Jack shouted to them, and they scurried away as the shooting increased.

Crouching low to the ground, Jack looked around for Reddy, but he was gone. Dodging bullets, Jack hurled himself behind a stack of wood. Reddy was already there, firing his gun with deadly accuracy at an unseen foe, following the burst of flame from their weapons.

"Took ya long enough t' get here," he drawled coolly between shots. "I didn't know how long ya was gonna stand out there and let 'em take potshots at ya."

Jack brought his gun up, aiming at a point of light across from him. A howl of pain ensued, and no more shots came from that spot.

"Did you see where Hank and Jake went to?" Jack asked.

"Naw, but ya can bet they're workin' their way in behind 'em," Reddy grunted. "Marshall and somebody else is firin' from that buildin' where the pris'ners are."

"Must be Toby—he sleeps in there to keep an eye out," Jack guessed. "Where's George?"

"He's pinned down behind that waterin' trough over there. Can ya hear his rifle? I been tryin' t' pick off the guy that's shootin' at 'im."

"Where's he at? I'll give it a try," Jack said, scooting over beside him.

"See that big tree just beyond the barn?" Reddy asked. "Watch t' the right of it. There! Did ya see it?"

Jack aimed at the spot and waited, firing almost simultaneously with the man's next shot. There was a cry, and the gun fell silent.

Suddenly, at the sound of more horses fleeing in the night, there was a pause in the shooting. Someone had driven off the attacker's mounts.

"Get out there and round up them nags!" came a bellow from the trees.

"Baxter Spriggs—the head of this party," Jack informed Reddy.

"Aaauggh!" was the only response as another of the attackers lost consciousness.

"Ah! Hank and Jake's out there gettin' 'em one by one," Reddy breathed. "Musta come up on their horses."

"Cover me," Jack said. "I don't want Spriggs to get away. I've got a score to settle with him."

"Don't move, Cap'n," Reddy ordered, surprising Jack by turning his gun on him. "Beggin' your pardon, sir, but ya ain't runnin' this show. You'll jest get yourself shot. Hank 'n' Jake won't know if you're a frien' or a foe. Jist ya sit right there and trust 'em t' do their work."

Disgusted with himself for letting Reddy get the drop on him, Jack could not help but admire the confidence the young man had in his partners. Hunkered there in the dark, he could only wait. A volley of shots came, then silence.

Soon three figures emerged from the woods. Baxter Spriggs was prodded forward by Hank and Jake. Reddy stood up and sheathed his gun.

"See—I told ya!" he exclaimed triumphantly.

About that time a shot rang out, making them all dive for cover. When all fell quiet, they emerged to find Spriggs laying spread-eagle, facedown on the ground. He was dead.

"Whoever he is, somebody wanted him dead," Mulholland grunted, rolling him over.

"It's Baxter Spriggs, Stant," Jack spoke up. "He gets his orders from higher up. Got kind of a mean streak too. Likes to beat innocent women and old people like Doc Steen. But for Cordelia Dureen, he would have murdered me when I was half dead with a bullet wound. They didn't want Spriggs talking."

"Where's Medford?" Mulholland asked, glancing around.

"I seen him go into the house," Toby said, walking toward them.

"Well, I guess everybody's been 'counted for," Mulholland said.

"Everyone except Jess, Stant," Jack said. "He was in the barn."

"Ya don't say—too bad!" Mulholland responded sadly, shaking his head. "He musta been the one that let them animals loose. That took a lotta guts. I can always use men like that." Turning to Hank, he said, "You men take care o' this fellow, then bring them others in so we can see what shape they're in.

"Ho—what's this?" he exclaimed, looking past Jack.

Jack turned to see Jess's roan walking slowing toward them. Only when he came to a stop a few feet away from them did they see the man clinging on his back. It was Jess, and Jack and Reddy jumped forward to catch him as he slid to the ground.

"Get him t' the porch, and I'll tell Medford t' bring a light," Mulholland ordered. Hank and Jake stepped in to help carry the injured man. Jess's shirt was covered with blood, letting the men know he had taken the first bullet. Still he had thought of the helpless animals before himself.

Under the light it was discovered Jess's burns were minimal, but the hair was singed on his head, and there was some blistering of his scalp. The bullet had grazed his flesh, just in from the armpit. A frightened Mantie came with hot water and bandages.

While Jack and Medford tended to Jess, the others saw to rounding up the horses that had stopped a short distance away. Prince had already returned to the yard, coming close to where Jack worked over the injured man. Because of the heroic action taken by Jess, the animals bore little evidence of injury, and once they were secured, the weary bunch of men turned in for the night.

*   *   *

The day of the meeting dawned with a hazy yellow sky and an uncanny stillness. Everything seemed held in suspension. Jack saddled Prince and led him out to where Medford and Mulholland were tightening the cinches on their saddles. The sight of Prince, high-stepping and prancing, brought the usual accolades from both men.

"He has the blood of the King in his veins," Jack said proudly. "If you think Prince is something, you should see Colonel Stothard's King."

Arriving at Dreyton Hall early, Medford and Mulholland joined Dreyton in welcoming the arriving guests, while Jack lingered in another room watching and listening. Crenshaw did not show up. This troubled Jack.

When it appeared no other guests were coming, Jack moved toward the drawing room, pausing just outside the door. Dreyton looked up to see him there. Jack caught Mulholland's eye and motioned to him. The marshall excused himself and came to join them.

"Stant, John says Crenshaw has never failed to show up when invited here," Jack said. "We probably ought to let John and George handle this while we ride into town to investigate. Crenshaw and the rest have probably caught wind of what's going on. What do you think?"

Mulholland agreed, "Crenshaw I want. We have the goods on him. The others we'll flush out later, once we get the goods on them. We'll get the meetin' goin', then let Dreyton carry on from there." He returned to the front with Dreyton while Jack followed, choosing a seat off to one side in the back.

"Gentlemen, if y'all will take a seat, we'll get started," Dreyton announced loudly to make his voice heard over the din of conversation. "We have here among us two distinguished men: U.S. Marshall Stanton Mulholland you've already met, and Captain Andrew Jackson Brevard, whom some of you have met before. I'm goin' to call on Captain Brevard to speak first."

Jack related the events leading up to the abduction of Cordelia Dureen and her subsequent rescue. "Now I'll let Marshall Mulholland or Mr. Medford tell you the rest," he concluded, returning to his seat.

The marshall chose to do the talking, telling of the attack at Medford's two nights ago. "Now, we've got some of 'em, but we don't know how many more's out there. This violence has gotta stop. It's gone too far 'n' it's a threat t' all of you. You need to take measures t' protect yourselves."

"What about the local sheriff?" one man asked.

"Mista Dreyton asked for help from the governor, and he sent me down. Your local sheriff is thought t' be in on the deal, 'n' we ain't takin' no chances. I hope we're wrong, but it's been known t' hap'n before. Now, ya'll excuse me because I've got some work t' do. Mista Dreyton 'n' Mista Medford'll answer your quest'ons from here on." Mulholland then headed for the door.

Jack let Prince set the pace down the lane. Marshall Mulholland's sturdy horse, though not much for looks, was no nag and kept neck to neck with Prince effortlessly.

Once outside the white-pillared gate, they raced along the wooded road leading toward the ferry. Rounding a bend, they were brought up short by the sight of a carriage off to one side of the road. The grazing horse reared its head to eye their cautious approach. Inside, they found bloodstains on the seat.

"I'd say som'body's pretty bad off, losing that much blood," Mulholland said. "Let's take a look aroun'."

"Stant, it's hard to say how far that horse traveled after the shooting," Jack noted.

"Yeah—you're probably right. Don't see a sign of a body here."

It was more than a mile before they found Crenshaw beside the trail in the tall grass. From the tracks, they could tell the horse had bolted, throwing Crenshaw from the carriage. He had been shot through the head several times. The small weapon he was wearing was still in its holster.

While the marshall examined the body, Jack searched the area for tracks. Hoofprints and a spent shell told him the assassin had fired at close range. Apparently Crenshaw knew the man and had not feared him. Jack picked up the shell casing and put it into his pocket. He would study it later.

"I'll ride back and get the carriage to put him in, Stant," he suggested. "Keep a sharp eye out."

Once they got Crenshaw aboard, Mulholland tied his horse behind the carriage and drove it back to Dreyton Hall, while Jack rode alongside. Pulling it to a halt before the stable, he handed the reins down to a stable hand, who came running. His eyes grew wide as he took in the gruesome sight of Crenshaw's body.

"Get Dreyton 'n' the others out here, quick!" Mulholland ordered as soon as his feet hit the ground.

Jack took care of their horses and joined him to wait for Dreyton and his guests, who poured from the house.

"What is it, Jack? What's up?" John Dreyton called, hurrying down the steps.

"Take a look, John," Jack answered, watching his face closely as his eyes fell upon Crenshaw. Only Dreyton, Medford, Mulholland, and Jack knew Crenshaw was coming to the meeting, unless Crenshaw had let it slip.

"It's Wilford Crenshaw! Where'd you find him?"

"Several miles down the road near that wooded area. He must have known who did it—his gun hadn't been drawn. Here's a shell from the gun that killed him."

"Looks like one from those revolvers we used in the war!" Dreyton exclaimed, as several crowded in close to take a look.

"Here—lemme see that," Mulholland said with authority, taking it from Dreyton's hand. "Army conscript, all right. Ain't a man here what wouldn't probab'ly have one aroun' the house."

He looked the group over with his piercing blue gaze.

"How many of ya came in by road this mornin'?"

"I reckon those of us who live on this side of the river, Marshall," one planter spoke up. "But we met 'n' rode along together. None of us laid eyes on a buggy on the road."

So intent were the circle of men around the marshall that no one noticed Jack Brevard slip into the stable.

"Humph—ya didn't, huh?" Mulholland responded, glaring at the portly planter sweating profusely in the heat.

"Musta' come along after us, Marshall," another man added.

"Didn't any of ya hear the shootin'?" Mulholland queried.

"No sir, Marshall. It was a quiet 'n' peaceful mornin'."

Mulholland turned to John Dreyton. "Who's his next o' kin?"

"I don't know if he had any," Dreyton answered. "He was a bachelor. Never heard him talk of any kin either."

"Well, never mind—I'll check on that later," Mulholland sighed, pulling out a big handkerchief to wipe the perspiration from his face. "When one of you men get back t' town, send out an undertaker t' pick up the body. Tell him I'll be stoppin' by t' talk t' him. I reckon I don't have t' tell ya'll t' go together, and don't be wanderin' off by yourselves. Ridin' alone is gettin' t' be unhealthy aroun' here."

The men expressed their appreciation to Dreyton for his hospitality and headed for their horses. Those going to

Charleston went to the waiting boat that had brought them across the Ashley.

Uneasy at what might be happening over at George Medford's place, Mulholland, Jack, and their host hit the trail for home. When they arrived, the marshall lingered behind to confront Jack.

"Why didn't ya tell me about the spent shell, Jack?" he asked with some irritation.

"No reason, Stant. I found it while I was looking at the tracks and put it in my pocket. Forgot it until later."

"What'd them tracks tell ya?" Mulholland asked, accepting Jack's explanation.

"Told me it was a big man of considerable weight sitting on that horse," Jack said with a thoughtful frown. "I checked the horses of the men there today, and though several of the planters had every reason to wish Crenshaw dead, they were telling the truth. None of their mounts made those tracks."

Stanton Mulholland thought about this bit of information for a moment. Jack Brevard had always been a good investigator. Had he told him all he knew?

"Do you want to know what I think, Stant?" Jack asked, as if he had read the marshall's mind.

"I think the man behind this whole thing intended to kill me, Cordelia Dureen, and Crenshaw. I think it's only a matter of time until he tries again."

"And ya think ya know who this man is?" asked Mulholland.

"I do."

"And ya intend to kill him, 'cause he's the same one who b'trayed ya?" Jack turned to pull the saddle from Prince's back, ignoring Mulholland's comment.

"Jack, that three pounds of iron strapped t' your hip don't give ya no cause to go shootin' a man," Mulholland argued in exasperation. "That'd be murder!"

"Then deputize me," Jack came back stubbornly.

"I've already got deputies here to take care of this job! Be reasonable!"

Jack walked away, leaving Mulholland standing there glaring after him. In the kitchen he found Mantie alone.

"How's Mrs. Dureen?"

"She ain't here."

"What do you mean, she isn't here?"

"She wuz worried 'bout her brother. She went o'er there."

"When?" he rasped, grabbing her arm.

"She left dis mornin' afta' ya'll did," Mantie answered, her eyes growing wide. "Nobody tol' her she can't!"

"How's Jess?"

"He's up 'n' aroun'."

"Where is he?"

"He's out checkin' on dem animals again," Mantie replied, indicating the direction with a swoop of her hand.

Jack went to find Jess in the makeshift corral. He seemed in good spirits and greeted Jack with enthusiasm.

"Hey dere, Cap'n. Look at dat ol' roan. He's as good as he can be afta dat singein' from de fire. Ain't dat de truth?"

Jack went in to look the horse over, noting little damage had been done to the smooth coat. "Reckon he'll do to ride, Jess. How's the shoulder?"

"Aw, it's 'most good as new, Cap'n. Kinda sore is all."

"Think you can ride?"

"Sho' do, Cap'n," Jess replied eagerly.

"Good!" Jack responded, looking around to see if anyone was near. Drawing close, he went on, "Get the horses ready and meet me out on the road after the others have turned in. Take care no one sees you. Do you understand? Have Mantie give you a bag of food to bring. We may be gone several days."

"Yes suh, ya kin count on ol' Jess. I be careful. Where we goin', Cap'n?"

"Clemson!" Jack hissed, turning away.

"Clemson!" Jess whispered under his breath, staring in wonder at the retreating figure.

Stalking off for the house, Jack looked up to see Mulholland standing on the porch watching him. Had he seen him talking with Jess? Probably. Before the marshall could speak, Jack addressed him cheerfully.

"Been out checking on Jess and his horse. It seems both are doing well after their close shave."

"Thet so?" Mulholland grunted, studying Jack's face as he drew closer. "From what I seen, looked like ya had a little secret goin' on betwixt ya."

"Aw, Stant, what makes you so suspicious of me?" Jack responded good-naturedly, flashing a disarming smile.

Mulholland lifted his hat to jam it down farther on his forehead. "I guess, Cap'n, it's 'cause I get the feelin' you're not playin' straight with me," he replied without emotion.

Jack silently took note Mulholland's remark held no warmth and caught its meaning. Stant was put out because he had left him in the dark about Clemson. No doubt his movements would be under surveillance from now on.

"Now, Stant, that's downright unfair!" Jack protested, feigning a wounded ego. "You've always known me to be a straight shooter."

"Yeah—we'll see," Mulholland admitted reluctantly. "It's been a long time, Jack."

Medford joined them, and the subject was dropped, but Jack found himself the object of Stanton Mulholland's thoughtful gaze more than once the rest of the day.

Toward evening Jack decided to test the extent to which he was being watched and strolled out to where Prince was in the corral. Toby was there feeding the other animals, which had been caught and penned up nearby.

"Evenin', Cap'n," he called over to Jack.

Jack walked over to him. "Hey there, Toby—are you doing all right?" he said loudly, then whispered, "Don't let on, but we're being watched."

"Yes suh!" Toby exclaimed, mumbling softly. "I see 'im."

"Toby, you've been around a lot. Do you know where I might find a man who built a big new house out here in the area?" Jack whispered. Out loud he asked, "Did Prince get a rubdown after I brought him in today?"

"He sho' did, Cap'n—I done it myself," the young man announced proudly.

Lowering his voice, Toby continued, "Dere's one been built south o' here in de low country. Ya can't miss it—sits high 'n' kin be seen fer miles around."

Jack heard a slight movement behind him. He turned to see Jake standing there, eyeing them suspiciously, his hand lingering near the gun strapped to his side.

"'Lo, Jake. Did you come to see about your horse too?" Jack greeted the deputy.

"Something like that," Jake replied. "I just wondered what all the commotion wuz."

Jack turned on his heel, heading for the house. So they were going to keep a close watch on him. Well, he would just have to find a way to give them the slip. His main concern was Jess. How would he be able to get the horses by such close scrutiny? Jack's mind raced as he sought for a plan to break free.

Supper was later than usual, and when they had all gathered around the table, the marshall announced he was going to pay a visit to the local sheriff the next day. If all went well, he would have the prisoners brought in there for safekeeping, relieving the burden from George Medford.

Jess came in with a bucket of water just in time to hear his comment and shot Jack a quick glance, not unnoticed by Mulholland. But when the marshall looked over at Jack, he seemed engrossed in some joke Reddy was telling. Maybe he was just jumpy, but somehow he had this feeling in his bones.

As WAS HIS HABIT, Jack remained on the porch long after the others had withdrawn to rest. Reddy joined him there, and the two of them talked for a long time. Finally, yawning and stretching sleepily, Jack announced he was going to turn in, leaving Reddy there in a rocking chair. But instead of going into his room, he merely opened and closed the door, then slipped out the back to circle the house. Reddy was standing on the porch with his back to him. Jack waited until Reddy stepped into the yard to head toward the back, then vanished into the moonless night.

True to his word, Jess was waiting out on the road in a clump of trees. They led the horses a ways before mounting up to ride away at a fast pace. Leaving the Ashley River road, they turned south toward the Edisto, riding hard. Both horses seemed to enjoy the freedom to run. On the short run the roan kept up but soon began to drop back, lacking the endurance of the big thoroughbred chestnut at his side. Jack held Prince in check to accommodate the roan's stride.

The ferry was on their side when they arrived at the river, and they thundered aboard. Once on the other side they rode silently, reigning in before Samuel's dark house. At Jess's knock, a light appeared quickly in response.

"Who be it?"

"Jess!" The sound of voices in the still night set off a chorus of barking dogs. The door opened, and they were quickly ushered into the kitchen, where a curtain of sorts was at the window.

Samuel set the lamp down onto the table and looked at them with questioning eyes.

"Jess needs a place to stay for a few days, Samuel—then we'll be on our way," Jack explained.

"And you, my friend?"

"I have a room waiting at Ravenswood's place. Jess will tell you all that's happened, and I'll see the two of you tomorrow."

Samuel turned the light down, and Jack slipped into the night to ride the short distance to Ravenswood's. Turning Prince loose in a stall, he removed his gear and headed for the house.

The door was unlocked, but he knocked anyway. Soon the door edged open to reveal Cressie's apprehensive face. Her face broke into a smile when she saw who it was.

"Who is it, Cressie?" Ravenswood called out from somewhere back in the house.

"It's Cap'n Jack, suh," she informed him, swinging the door open for Jack to enter.

"Is that you, Jack?"

"Yes, Sandy—I need a place to stay for a few days."

"Ya know where your room is" was the reply.

"Thanks—we'll talk in the morning," Jack promised, heading up the stairs with the lamp Cressie gave him.

At breakfast the next morning Jack filled in Ravenswood on all that had happened since they had last talked. When he came to the part about Cordelia's abduction, tears came to Ravenswood's eyes, and his emotions ran from concern to anger, then finally thankfulness. When Jack had finished, Ravenswood sat silent and thoughtful.

"Jack, I'm sorry," he said finally. "I misjudged ya, and I apologize. I thought you was out fer revenge fer revenge's sake. Now I'm lookin' at it different. I'm glad ya caught the ones that carried out the order, and if I wasn't half a man, I'd go after the one behind all this m'self!"

Jack pushed back his plate and got to his feet. "Sandy, John sent for a U.S. marshall to come down to help out. You'd never guess who he is. Do you remember Stanton Mulholland? He was in our regiment."

"Big fella. Yes, I do remember 'im. Yer sayin' he's a U.S. marshall? Well, whatta ya know?"

"I told him you were down here. He was mighty glad to hear you made it."

"Be nice if he'd drop down whilst in the area," Ravenswood said eagerly.

"I'll tell him," Jack promised, picking up his hat.

Ravenswood followed him to the door, his wooden leg thumping along on the hard floor. "You'll be back?" he asked.

"I'll be back if . . . ," Jack promised with a grave expression, leaving the rest unsaid.

"Jack," Ravenswood began, placing a hand on his arm, "you'll be careful?"

"Say a prayer for me, Sandy," Jack responded, touched by the man's concern.

*   *   *

Jess was ready when Jack arrived, and they headed out. Toby had said the place was easy to see. That meant it must be set on a knoll or incline. They rode for some time without spotting it. Taking a more westerly direction, they were rewarded with a spectacular setting. The pretentious house sat high on a picturesque rise in the ground with white fences and a pond in the foreground.

"So that's Clemdenin Hall," Jack muttered to himself.

"Fo' sho' ya ain't seen nuttin' like dat!" Jess exclaimed.

Jack led the way into a clump of trees so they could observe the activity without being seen. Other than workers in the fields and a man taking care of the stock, things looked quiet.

"Huh!" Jack grunted. "I guess now is as good a time as any, Jess. We'll circle around and come in from that side over there." Jack pointed to a spot where the trees came out in a point toward the outer buildings off to their left. "Keep a sharp eye out, and don't be fooled by the peaceful front," he warned, urging Prince forward. "We could be riding into an armed camp."

Amazed at how easy it was to reach the house, the two secured their horses at a hitching post on the back side of the building and went forward toward the wide porch surrounding that side. Jack pulled his gun and stepped through the open door into the kitchen. Pots were steaming on the woodstove, but no one was around. He could hear voices in a small pantry off to the side.

Directly across from him was a door leading to the interior of the house. He headed for it with Jess close behind. On the other side, he found himself in a spacious, elaborately decorated hall, with arches rising to the ceiling, supporting a huge chandelier. Off to the right, double doors led into another room. A slight sound of movement there directed his steps that way. Motioning for Jess to wait just outside the door, Jack entered to find a man working at a desk with his back toward him. In a mirror before the desk, Jack could see the bespeckled face of the man who had betrayed him. All the bitterness he had harbored for so long returned, and he felt he was sliding down a steep hill with no way to stop himself.

Ravenswood's words echoed in his mind: "The war was awful . . . what yer thinkin' 'bout now will be murder."

Only when Clemson laid aside the papers he was working on did he look into the mirror to see Jack standing over him. His sallow face blanched, and the pen in his hand fell to the floor.

"Jack Brevard! After—all these years!" he managed to get out. "I've wondered many times where you were."

"Well, you don't have to wonder anymore," Jack ground out, pulling the chair around. "Get up!"

"What—do you intend—to do?" the stricken man panted, without moving to obey.

"Settle something that should have been settled long ago," Jack said coldly, clutching at him. "Get up!"

The covering that had been on his lap slipped to the floor, revealing twisted, arthritic legs. Crutches leaned against the wall by the desk, and nearby was a wheelchair. Jack's mind whirled as the truth slowly dawned on him: Clemson was crippled! He couldn't get up! He lowered his gun and stepped back, staring wild-eyed at the man he had hated for so long.

"All these years I've wanted to say I'm sorry, Jack, but I didn't know where you were," Clemson quavered, lifting a shaking, misshapen hand. "Will you forgive me as God has forgiven me?"

Before Jack could reply, Jess stepped into the room behind him. "Cap'n, someone's comin'," he said. Then his eyes fell on Clemson. "Cap'n, dat ain't Clemson!"

"What are you saying, Jess? This is Clemson, the man who betrayed me and left me to rot while my mother died of a broken heart!" Jack responded, his voice breaking.

"Dat might be, Cap'n, but he ain't dat nightridin' man what stole Mantie 'n' killed my pa!"

Jack turned numb. His hatred for Clemson had almost made him kill the wrong man! Sandy Ravenswood's words echoed in his brain: "Vengeance is mine; I will repay, saith the Lord." Certainly Clemson looked as if he had suffered enough.

"It's settled, Clemson—live in peace," he said abruptly, the anger draining from him.

Footsteps sounded in the hall, and Jack heard a familiar voice: "Clemmy, I thought I heard voices. Is—"

Jack spun around to find Cordelia Dureen standing in the doorway staring from one to the other, trying to comprehend the meaning of his presence.

"Jack! What—," her voice stopped at the sight of the gun in his hand.

Jack plunged past her and ran to where Prince stood waiting. Jumping into the saddle, he sped away, leaving Jess to catch up with him.

Jess found him sitting alongside of the road, head in hands.

"Ya lookin' like a sittin' duck," Jess said, slipping from the saddle to come stand by his side.

"I came within a little of killing her brother, Jess," Jack muttered thickly. "How can she ever forgive me?"

"Maybe she don't know, Cap'n."

"She'll know," Jack said with finality, getting to his feet. "I guess what is to be is to be. Let's ride."

While they waited for the ferry, Jack recalled what Jess had said when he saw Clemson.

"Jess, you said that man wasn't Clemson as you know him. What does this man who calls himself Clemson look like?"

"Ain't never seen his face, Cap'n. He's careful 'bout dat. He's a big man, dough. Kinda sits on his hoss hunkered over, hangs over in de shoulders; don't say much. Lets dat Spriggs fella do his talkin'."

A vivid picture of a big man sitting just out of the circle of light came to Jack's remembrance. He had seen the man the night they tried to lynch Jess at his father's place. But why was he posing as Clemson?

"Do you remember anything about what he wore—hat or boots?"

"Nuttin' onusual. His hat wuz black 'n' his boots too. Only thing—he always had a cigar in his mouth."

The ferry arrived, ending the conversation, but later that night at Ravenswood's Jack lay awake trying to piece things together. Someone was impersonating Clemson, but who? The plausible answer would be someone who wanted to get Clemson out of the way.

Jack bolted up in the bed. Of course: Tom Searles! Searles had gone to great lengths to make Jack think he was an invalid. Counting on Jack's promise to hunt Clemson down and kill him that night of their capture by the Union soldiers, Searles had set him up to commit murder. With Jack in prison for life or hung, and with Clemson dead, Searles and his nightriders could go on with a respectable cover for their evil deeds. When Jack took so long to carry out his plan, Searles had become wary and tried to have him killed.

The attack on George Medford's place was not just happenstance. Searles intended to get him at any cost. Fortunate for them, Searles had not known of the presence of the marshall and his deputies. He must have been there in the trees that night. It would have been he who shot Spriggs to keep him from talking.

Jack left his bed and walked to the window. Out there a few miles away was the brave woman who had stolen his heart. Why had she become a target? Could it be Searles learned the connection between her and Clemson and tried to get rid of her by making it look as though she was being held for ransom?

Fear for Cordelia's safety swept over him, and Jack realized she was exactly where she should not be at this moment. By this time Searles would be a desperate man. That thought spurred him into action. Jack hurriedly strapped on his gun, then grabbed his hat and boots, carrying them in his hand down the stairs to keep from waking the household. Outside he pulled them on and ran for the stable. His mind raced as he saddled Prince. Although he hated to take the time to get Jess, he knew one more hand could make a difference.

*   *   *

Stanton Mulholland was furious the next morning when he found Jack had given him the slip and guessed it had something to do with Cordelia's leaving. To fail to see that Brevard was in love with her, one would have to be blind. But why had he taken Jess with him?

Jake reported he had seen Brevard talking to Toby just before dark. When Toby was summoned, he told them the captain had asked about the new place and the way to get there.

"Who was he goin' t' see there?" the marshall asked. When Toby hesitated, he roared, "Speak up, man!"

"Clemson," Toby whispered, looking from one to the other. "He's de one what's 'sponsible fo' all dis trouble."

So what John Dreyton told him was true, the marshall admitted to himself with a sigh. Jack Brevard was going after his old enemy. He had hoped Dreyton was wrong. Well, he would just have to chase him down. That would mean he would have to postpone taking the prisoners into town for a while.

"Hank, you 'n' Reddy saddle up," he ordered, "'n' bring up my horse too. Jake, you're stayin' here t' help guard the pris'ners."

Mulholland lifted his large frame out of his chair and stalked out to find George Medford, who was supervising the cleanup from the fire.

"Medford, me 'n' some of my men are goin' t' be gone for a few days. I'm leavin' Jake here t' help wi' them pris'ners. 'Pears like somethin's come up t' keep me from gettin' 'em off your hands."

"Don't worry 'bout it, Marshall—we'll manage," Medford assured him cheerfully.

An hour later, Mulholland and his men rode up the wide avenue to Clemson's impressive home. Leaving the men to care for the horses and keep watch, the marshall ascended the open-arm stairway leading to the wide veranda. The maid answered his knock, inviting him to wait in the large hall.

Cordelia appeared shortly, looking lovely in a long blue dress against the backdrop of gold and white splendor.

"Marshall, welcome to our home!" she said graciously. "My brother is in the drawing room. Come this way."

Introducing Mulholland to her brother, Cordelia settled into a chair opposite him and waited for him to speak.

"Ya have a nice place here, Mista Clemson. 'Bout as fine as I've ever seen, 'ceptin' the governor's mansion. Ya've done well."

"I'm very grateful for what I have, sir," Clemson replied. "I had planned to build in the North, but as you can see, the weather there would be very hard on my condition."

Cordelia listened to the small talk, wondering what the marshall was really there for. Therefore, she was not surprised when Captain Brevard's name came up.

"I hear we have a mutual friend, Clemson, by the name of Jack Brevard."

Clemson glanced at his sister, noting her heightened color. "Yes, I believe we do," he responded. "Jack was by earlier this morning to see me. We had some old fences to mend, as you no doubt have heard. I made a mistake years ago that resulted in a lot of suffering for him. I was glad to get it off my chest."

"Ya don't know he came here t' kill ya? He thinks you're behind all the killin' 'n' raidin'."

"I find that hard to believe, sir," Clemson said with a chuckle, "since you can see, as well as he, that I am incapable of getting around without help."

Mulholland felt instinctively that the man was lying, but he decided to let that part of the matter go.

"Did he say where he was goin'?"

"No sir, but I wouldn't be a bit surprised if Jack Brevard doesn't track the man who was responsible for the insults heaped on my sister," Clemson said with spirit. "For that I will be eternally grateful."

"I take it she's told ya of his darin' rescue?"

"Certainly."

"Does that have anythin' to do with ya lyin' t' protect him?"

Cordelia was proud of her brother at that moment as he drew himself up in his chair to look the marshall straight in the eye. "Marshall, I have always known Jack Brevard to be a brave and honorable man. I did him wrong, and the guilt I've carried these many years has taken its toll on me physically and mentally. Today I got rid of my guilt and the bitterness. Only now can I have the peace I've longed for."

Marshall Mulholland turned to Cordelia, and she felt his intense gaze trying to penetrate her thoughts.

"Ya know the man's in love with ya?" he said bluntly.

"I am aware of it," she answered honestly, lowering her head as a blush crept into her face.

"I know it's none of my business, ma'am, but—do you love him?"

"Yes," she whispered, raising her eyes to meet his. "And not only I, Marshall, but everyone, both black and white, for whom he's been willing to sacrifice his life."

Mulholland stared at the floor for a long time with a furrowed brow. He had always had a great respect for Brevard and regretted that he had misjudged him. If Clemson was not the man responsible for the killings, he would have to ferret out whoever it was. Jack no doubt already knew. His only hope was to get there in time.

Pushing himself to his feet, Mulholland looked down at Cordelia Dureen. Jack Brevard was a very fortunate man to have the love of such a woman.

"Ma'am," he said gently, "when do you expect Jack t' be back?"

"I don't know," she answered with a slight frown. "He was in a hurry when he left."

Mulholland saw a shadow pass across her violet gaze and wondered. He hesitated as if about to say something, then changed his mind and walked to the door.

"Marshall, it's growing late—you're welcome to stay the night," his host spoke up hopefully. "We'd be more than glad to have you, and there's plenty of room."

Mulholland glanced at the slanting rays of the sun. If they started right away, it would be late when they arrived back at Medford's. The offer of a bed didn't sound all that bad.

"I'd be much obliged, Clemson, but there's three of us, 'n' we don't want t' be no trouble."

"No trouble, sir. Turn your horses into the barn and Cordelia will see that three plates are added at the table. We eat at sundown."

*   *   *

In the darkness it was harder to find the lane to Clemson's house. Finally Jack located it and rode up under the shelter of one of the many giant live oak trees lining the broad approach.

"We'll leave the horses here and go on foot," he whispered to Jess. "Keep your eyes and ears open."

They kept close to the fence as they crept forward, stopping at intervals to listen. Jack headed for the point of trees he had used the day before. Pausing to listen and choose a course of action, he froze at a familiar sound. It was the unmistakable stamp of a horse. Laying a hand of restraint on Jess's arm, Jack strained every sense to detect the presence of another human being. He could make out the vague outline of the horse off to his left.

"Cover me," he whispered to Jess, cautiously making his way in that direction.

The animal raised its head, but fortunately it did not give away his presence. Up close, he inspected the outfit in the dim light of the stars, and what he found turned his blood cold. The horse belonged to Tom Searles.

Frantically, Jack retraced his steps to where Jess waited. Motioning him to follow, he made for the house, staying in the shadows of the outbuildings. The last 50 feet to the house was in the open, shadowed only by a large tree just off the porch. Searching every dark corner for sign of movement, Jack saw none. That would mean Searles had gained entrance to the house.

"I seen someone lightin' a smoke out on de front porch," Jess breathed in his ear.

"Is he still there?"

"He wuzn't movin'."

"Let's go," Jack whispered, leading off at a fast run.

Reaching the house without being detected, Jack found the door ajar. They entered, moving softly across the kitchen to the door going into the great hall.

"Wait here," he whispered to Jess.

The door to the drawing room was slightly open, sending a shaft of light across the shining floor. Jack tiptoed his way toward it. Voices were heard in the room beyond, then a gasp, followed by a thud. What he saw through the crack of the door chilled his blood. Tom Searles was bending over Clemson's prostrate body on the floor. He despaired he had arrived too late, but a quick glance around the room led him to believe Cordelia was not there. While Jack pondered what course of action to take, Searles picked up a lamp, gave Clemson one last look, and came toward him.

Jack stepped back into the shadow of one of the arches. Searles was in such a hurry he did not pause to look around but made straight for the stairs. He was going for Cordelia! Jack stepped out, pulling his gun. At the click of the hammer, Searles froze.

"Hello, Tom. I see your legs are better."

"Jack!" Searles responded with some relief, turning to face him. "Yeah—new medicine," he lied, his eyes searching the dim corners of the hall to see if they were alone. He turned a baleful gaze back on Jack. "If you've come to take care of Clemson, yer too late."

"I know, Tom. Unbuckle your gun belt! Now!" Jack ordered when Searles hesitated.

Out of the corner of his eye, he saw Cordelia come to the top of the stairs, dark hair cascading around her shoulders.

"Jack!" she gasped. Then her wondering gaze fell on Searles standing on the stairs, and her face turned white as she read the meaning of his presence there.

"Get back, Cordelia, quick!" Jack ordered without taking his eyes off Searles.

With a cry, Cordelia ran to her room, closing the door. Jess moved in behind Jack, "Dat's him!" he cried accusingly. "He's de one what stole Mantie 'n' killed my pappy! Dat's Clemson!"

Shouts and the sound of running footsteps could be heard outside as someone sounded the alarm. Searles hurled the lamp at Jack and turned to run up the stairs. Ducking the burning missile, Jack fired his weapon, but the bullet missed its target. The lamp exploded upon impact, sending kerosene on the draperies and across the floor. The flames spread greedily, sending heavy smoke through the hall. Jack leaped the fire in pursuit of Searles just as Mulholland stormed in with Hank and Reddy on his heels.

"What's goin' on here?" he thundered.

"Cap'n's after dat man Searles what calls hisself Clemson!" Jess yelled above the crackle of the flames. His voice became hysterical as a woman's scream rent the air. "He's gonna hurt Miz Cordelia. Dey's up dere somewhere. Ya gotta help 'im!"

"Reddy, get outside and keep a watch for anybody comin' from a window!" Mulholland ordered, skirting the fire to gain the steps. "Hank, try t' find Mista Clemson 'n' get him outta here! Jess, try t' put this fire out!"

A threatening voice led Jack to an open door. What he saw stopped him cold. Searles had a stranglehold on Cordelia, using her as a shield. Jack could only watch helplessly, unable to fire his weapon for fear of hitting her.

"Drop yer gun, Jack, or I'll choke the breath from her," Searles snarled, tightening his grip on her neck.

"Tom, let her go," Jack said coldly. "Let this be between you and me!"

"I'm no match fer you, Jack—blast yer hide, I never was! Now drop yer gun, and step back!" Searles gave Cordelia's neck a cruel jerk.

Neither man saw Mulholland standing there. When Jack's weapon hit the floor, the marshall stepped into the shadows of a nearby doorway, crouching down to escape the thick layer of smoke forming above him. Jack moved backward from the room, giving Searles access to the stairs.

"Back off down there—he's got Cordelia!" he yelled down to Hank and Jess, who were fighting a losing battle with the fire. "Let him out!"

The men dropped their wet gunnysacks and stepped away. Releasing his stranglehold on Cordelia's neck, Searles made his way sideways down the steps, dragging her with him. Hank stood with his hand in the air. Jess had disappeared into the smoke.

"You'll never make it through the fire, Searles, unless you jump," the deputy warned, trying to keep the crazed man's attention. Out of the corner of his eye, Hank saw his boss edge out behind Searles.

Searles hesitated, searching for a way of escape from the flames below him. Cordelia saw her chance and bit Searles on the hand, kicking and biting until he flung her free. Throwing herself over the banister, she hung there momentarily, afraid to let go. Searles pointed his gun at her, and she stared panic-stricken at the small round hole that was meant to end her life.

"Searles!" came Mulholland's thunderous cry.

She let go just as a flash of fire came from the barrel. She fully expected to hit the hard floor below. Instead, she fell into someone's arms.

"It be all right now, Miz Cordelia," she heard Jess say.

Overhead there was the roar of guns and someone's stricken cry. Then she lost consciousness.

15

CORDELIA BECAME AWARE she was lying on the ground, and there was a burning in her lungs as she tried to breathe. She came to, coughing and gasping for air. Someone lifted her up to cradle her in his arms. Opening her eyes, she saw Jack's face over her. Tears were running unashamedly down his face. Behind him was Jess, worried and wild-eyed. A big smile of relief wreathed his black face when he saw her eyes open.

"Dere she is, sho' nuff!" he exclaimed happily. "See? I told ya she wuz gonna be all right."

"Thank God," Jack responded, laying her back gently.

"Searles?" she asked with a strangled whisper.

"Mulholland just winged him, and Hank fished him from the fire," Jack informed her. "He'll live to stand trial."

Cordelia pushed herself up to look wildly around. What was left of the once-beautiful home lay in angry, glowing coals against a backdrop of darkness. People she had never seen milled around the yard. Mulholland left his men to work on the wounded Searles and walked over to where she lay. His face brightened when he saw her awake. She looked at him with questioning eyes.

"My—my brother?"

Mulholland shifted his gaze to Jack and bowed his head. Cordelia turned her violet gaze to Jack's face, reading the truth there. Scalding tears rushed to her eyes.

"He didn't—the fire—?"

"No, it was Searles," Jack answered. "Hank brought him out."

"Why—did Searles—do this to us?" she choked out.

"Searles, your brother, and I escaped from a Union prison together. Your brother was the one who betrayed us. Searles was sent to Perryville, and I was returned to the prison, while your brother went free."

"My brother—was the man you came to kill, wasn't he?" she pressed.

"Yes," Jack admitted, his voice faltering before her direct gaze. Then he went on: "I was very bitter about what happened to my parents and the suffering I was forced to endure, and I pledged I would hunt him down. When Searles wrote that Clemson was here in the area, I came. Searles pretended he was crippled and told me I would have to settle the score for both of us. He blamed all the killings on Clemson. I decided to investigate for myself. Everyone I talked to told me the man's name was Clemson.

"That day when I came to find your brother, the truth dawned on me at last. It was then I realized Tom Searles was counting on my hate to destroy Clemson and clear the way for himself. I would go to prison for the murder, and he would join the respectable community.

"When he began to suspect I was on to him, he tried to kill me. That's what brought you into the picture. The rest of the story you know."

Cordelia stared off into the night for what seemed like an eternity, then, turning her gaze back to his face, she said, "Jack, I have to know. What was the real reason you didn't—you spared by brother?"

"It was something my father said many years ago and others have repeated: 'Vengeance is mine; I will repay, saith the Lord.' Your brother had suffered enough, and when I saw him there, all the bitterness left me. We made our peace. One thing I want you to know, Cordelia—I did not know he was your brother until then."

Jack waited for Cordelia to speak. When no response came, he got to his feet and walked into the night. Jess followed shortly, to find Jack standing with one arm over Prince's neck in sad contemplation. No word was spoken as they mounted up and rode away.

The eastern sky was announcing a new day when they rode in at George Medford's, weary and spent. Lamplight shone from a window in the kitchen. The men turned their horses into the corral and headed that way. Medford and Jake were huddled over a cup of coffee when they entered. Mantie was working over the stove, preparing breakfast.

"Well, you two look like ya need some rest!" Medford greeted pleasantly. "Mantie, bring some coffee. We'll have somethin' t' eat in a few minutes. Pull up a chair."

Jack brought forward a chair, while Jess perched on a stack of wood by the stove to chat with Mantie.

"Where's Mulholland?" Jake asked.

Tired as he was, while they ate their meal Jack filled them in briefly on what had happened. He then sought his bed.

* * *

More than a week had passed. Jack had tried to fill the empty days. This particular morning he picked up his cup and went to sit listlessly on the back porch. Medford and Jess had eaten earlier and were busy repairing some posts at the corral. Marshall Mulholland had come for his prisoners, and he and his men were gone. Jack had hoped for a message from Cordelia but was disappointed. All Mulholland told him was that she had sent for John Dreyton to come and take her to her home in Charleston. The fact she had turned to Dreyton for help and had returned to town confirmed what he already knew, Jack thought gloomily: Cordelia could not forgive him after all.

It was time he moved on, he decided sadly, tossing the cold coffee from his cup. Nothing would be gained by sitting here licking his wounds. Tomorrow he would leave for Georgia.

As Medford left Jess and headed for the house, Jack waited for his approach. "Mornin', Jack—why so glum?" Medford hailed, studying the face of his friend as he lifted his hat to wipe the perspiration from his forehead.

"I'm moving on in the morning, George," Jack announced. "I've been meaning to talk with you."

"Where ya headed?"

"I'm going back to Georgia. Think I'll look up the land my father owned. Don't know what I'll find."

"Ya takin' Jess with ya?"

"If he wants to go. If all goes well, we'll send for Mantie later, if it's all right with you. She's in no condition to travel until after the baby comes, anyway."

"It's too bad she has to bear that man's baby," Medford observed.

"Searles wasn't so bad in the beginning, George. The war changed people—some for the better, others for the worse. I didn't appreciate what my parents instilled in me as a boy. I was stubborn, and it took me a long time to see it. Before now I've never wanted to go back."

"Those of us here are sure beholdin' t' ya', Jack," Medford said with feeling. "Take care of yourself, son. It's men like you what'll rebuild the South. Wife 'n' I will keep ya in our prayers."

"I'm going to need them, George," Jack replied brokenly, taking a deep shaking breath. "It's not going to be easy."

"Cordelia loves ya, Jack, 'n' she's true blue. It's just, well, she's been through a lot. Given time, she'll come around."

Jack shook his head. "I almost killed her brother, George—she'll never forgive me for that," he said flatly.

"The woman has a big heart, Jack. I'm countin' on her love for ya t' bring ya both through. Besides, the Maker didn't intend for ya t' be a murderer, 'n' in His great plan He worked it all out."

When Jack remained in thoughtful silence, Medford went on: "How'll I be able t' get in touch with ya? When the crops come in, I want t' send ya payment on what I owe."

"I'll get word to you," Jack answered quietly, getting to his feet to head out to where Jess was working.

*   *   *

While Jess waited with the horses, Jack entered a modest building on the east side of Atlanta. An overhead sign read, "Cornwallis D. Shales, esq." Shales had been one of his father's most trusted friends. Jack felt sure he would know of his father's actions in those last days before the fall of Atlanta.

The man behind the desk had aged noticeably, but Jack would have known him anywhere. A tall, slender man with bony frame and angular jaw, Shales finished what he was writing before looking up. His cavernous eyes set beneath bushy brows expressed genuine pleasure when he realized who Jack was.

"Jack Brevard!—is that you?" he said with enthusiasm, getting up to come around the desk with his hand reaching out to Jack in greeting. "Last I heard, at your father's funeral, you were in prison. I'd just about given up on ever hearing from you again. Where've you been?"

"Since the war, I've been down in the Savannah area and other parts," Jack replied, taking the chair Shales indicated. "This is the first I've been back this way for a long time."

"Have you been out by the homeplace?"

"No, I thought I'd come by to talk with you first," Jack answered, lowering his eyes to watch a fly skate across his boot. "I—didn't know but what someone else may be living there."

"Shouldn't be," Shales assured him, turning to unlock a drawer. He took out an oilskin packet and handed it to Jack. "Your father left this with me shortly before he died, with the instructions to give it to you if you ever came back."

Staring at the familiar packet, Jack felt the blood leave his face as he remembered his father's words that day he had first seen it. The elder Brevard had taken him into his room to unlock a strongbox he had always kept beneath his bed. Taking out the packet, he had explained what its contents were: "I always meant this land to go to my sons. Jack, stay and help me work it. There are others to fight the war. If you go, Jim will go too!"

Too late Jack had come home to fill his father's wishes. All were gone, he thought sadly. He looked up to see Shales watching him with a curious expression.

"Is something wrong?"

Jack wiped his hand across his eyes. "It's just—well—dealing with memories from the past is hard. I—"

"It's been difficult for all of us, son, but we owe it to their memory to rebuild the South to what they dreamed it would be." Shale rose to his feet to come to Jack, placing a hand on his shoulder.

"Jack, I predict you will see a great city rise from the ashes here. Already it's begun!" he exclaimed. "There's new hope and construction everywhere! Young men like you will add to the stability of the South during these troublesome times of restoration. I'm mighty glad to see you back, and if there's anything I can help you with, let me know."

"Thank you, Mr. Shales—I just may have to call on you," Jack returned with a smile, getting to his feet. "Good day."

After picking up supplies at a small general store, Jack led the way out the familiar road toward the old homeplace. Though the road and the landscape were still the same, chimneys standing over charred remains of homes were grim reminders of the war. The owners had either moved on or been killed. With the hot afternoon sun bearing down upon their backs, Jack and Jess sought refuge in the shade of a large tree to rest the horses and eat a cold biscuit.

"How much we have t' go yet?" Jess asked, glancing up the winding red clay road.

"Not far," Jack replied, his voice thick with emotion.

After seeing the devastation of houses along the way, Jack dreaded what he would find ahead. Jess noted his preoccupation and ate the rest of his meager lunch in silence.

Soon on their way again, Jack rode Prince at a faster pace, slowing only when they approached a gentle knoll. Had he not recognized the giant tree standing at the entrance, he would have ridden on past the dim trail hidden in the undergrowth.

His heart was full as he rode in between the pine trees lining each side. The pine saplings he and his brother had bent over to ride as horses against an imaginary enemy had grown into tall, crooked trees. As he came into the open, the first thing he saw was the massive chimney standing like a bleak, lonely sentinel over the charred remains of what was once home.

Echoes of the past rang in his ears as he rode forward with a heavy heart. The horse's hoofbeats made a hollow sound on the wooden bridge spanning the clear stream running beneath. In its waters he and his younger brother had played, catching minnows and splashing on hot days.

From its lofty perch in a live oak tree, a mockingbird sang out its welcome when they rode into the yard. The devastation was complete, except for a small house old Hiram had lived in. Jack reflected sweetly on his memories of the blind elderly black man who once lived there.

Overwhelmed with a deep sense of grief, Jack urged Prince forward. Jess silently followed, sensing this was no time to speak. Had he not gone through the same thing?

They dismounted before the tiny dwelling, and Jess explored its possibilities while Jack walked through the rubble that was once a home filled with warm and loving people.

When Jess returned to the porch, Jack stood with head bowed, outlined against late afternoon sky. Then Jess saw him do a strange thing: he lifted his hands toward the heavens, and with his face turned to the sky, he gave a wild, exultant cry. Had he been with Jack in battle, Jess would have heard the same response as he met the enemy. With squared shoulders, Jack strode forcefully toward him, face gleaming in the light.

"Tomorrow we'll start to rebuild, Jess. Right now, we'll see about setting up some quarters." With renewed vigor, he added, "What'd you find in there?"

"Not much. Ever'thin's gone. But leastways it's a roof o'er our haids."

In the days and weeks following, Jack hired a crew of men to assist Jess in clearing the land and repairing the foundation of the house. Then slowly but surely the walls of the house rose into being. Jack built the spacious dwelling to have verandas all around and large rooms with windows opening to the porches, providing good ventilation and view. In all his planning he saw a lovely face with dark eyes. Yet in the lonely nights, he struggled. What right had he to expect she would ever come? Still, day after day he worked hopefully with her in mind, pausing for long intervals to stare toward the road.

Fall faded into a mild winter as work on the house continued. With the coming of spring, the main house was finished except for the hanging of doors, and the barn was nearing completion. Peach trees his father had planted were coming to life with promising bloom, and the trimmed hedges and shrubs were putting on a new mantle of green.

Jack had grown lean and brown now, with no noticeable effects from his gunshot wounds. With a little more leisure time, he became a forlorn figure, withdrawing more and more as he became locked into loneliness. Evenings were spent in agonizing reverie. What was the joy of a fine home if there was no loving companion there to share it?

Jess accepted this change in his friend with great understanding, for he himself found his thoughts returning to Crawfish's granddaughter Cally. Would she return his affection? Using his spare time to make the little house comfortable, Jess vowed he would go see her when he returned for Mantie.

The day soon came when Jess hammered the last shingle into place. Picking up his nails, he came down the ladder to where Jack stood waiting for him.

"Well, dat jest 'bout do it, Cap'n," he announced cheerfully, laying his tools down to wipe the sweat from his dark face. "I's been wonderin'—do ya reckon it be 'bout time we oughta fetch Mantie?"

"I've been thinking on that, Jess," Jack answered slowly. "We could use a woman around the place. Why don't you take one of the wagons and go for her while I stay here and keep an eye on things? There's no reason for me to go, except for George. I'll send a letter with you for him."

Watching Jack walk away, Jess began to form a plan in his mind. While he was in the Charleston area, he would go see Miz Cordelia. "Somebody's gotta do somethin'!" he muttered, shaking his head sadly. "The cap'n's pinin' away for his woman, 'n' it looks like ol' Jess is gonna hafta take de bull by de horns."

*   *   *

Jack ran his hand over the edge of the door he was planing and straightened up to clean the shavings from the blade. Jess had been gone for nearly a month, and he was getting worried.

Shading his eyes, Jack searched the wooded lane as he had done many times the past few days. There was no movement in sight. If Jess did not come before he hung this last door, he would have to go in search of him, he decided, returning to his work.

Two days later, Jack fitted the hinges together and slipped the pin into place. He stepped back to survey his work, opening and closing the door, which swung freely. With a grunt of satisfaction, he gathered up his tools. Though he had never taken a liking to carpentry, Jack had nevertheless admitted a deep appreciation for the patient training his father had given to an ungrateful son.

It was almost dark when Jack heard the sound of a wagon coming along the lane. Walking around to the front, he beheld a strange sight emerge from the shelter of the trees. A wagon covered with canvas was making its way toward him. At the reins was Jess, and he let out a whoop and waved his hat at the sight of Jack. A smiling Cally was at his side.

"Hey dere, Cap'n! We done fin'ly got here!"

Jack waited until the wagon drew nearer before answering, "It sure took you long enough, Jess. I was just about to come looking for you!"

Jess pulled the wagon to a stop before the house and set the brake. Tying the reins, he jumped to the ground and reached for Cally.

"Where's Mantie?" Jack asked.

"She's ridin' in de wagon wi' Toby," Jess responded with a mysterious air, pointing at the second wagon coming up the lane. "Dey's comin' along."

Jack stepped aside as a beaming Toby pulled the second wagon to a stop beside the other.

"Cap'n, it sho' is good t' see ya—looks like you 'n' Jess is been busy, sho' nuff," Toby greeted him, his eyes taking in the buildings. "Dat is sho' some kinda house!"

There was movement inside, and Mantie stuck a smiling face through the flap. "Ev'nin' Cap'n. Is 'at husband of mine feedin' ya a line?"

"Be still, woman, 'n' hand dat youngun down here," Toby retorted good-naturedly, holding his arms out to her.

Mantie pulled in her head to return in a moment with a bundle to hand to Toby. Cally stepped forward to take the baby while Toby assisted Mantie from the wagon. She pulled back the coverlet to reveal a tiny face that wrinkled into a frown at being disturbed.

"Cap'n, meet Andrew Jackson," Cally said proudly.

"I wanted him t' have your name, Cap'n," Mantie said shyly. "You've been s' good to me 'n' Jess."

"Thank you, Mantie," Jack responded warmly. "I trust I'll be a good example."

Suddenly everyone fell silent as if not knowing what to say next. Jess cleared his throat loudly and turned to the task of unloading the wagon.

"We best be gettin' de stuff from dis wagon befo' it gits too dark," he stated with authority.

Jack followed to lay a restraining hand on his arm. "Jess, did you—uh—was there any word from—uh, Charleston—I mean—," Jack asked quietly, floundering for words.

"Mista Medford sent ya some money, Cap'n," Jess answered with feigned innocence, knowing full well the captain was asking about Cordelia. "It be in a pouch under the seat."

Jack hid his disappointment by offering to give them a hand. Jess and Toby exchanged glances then exhorted him to show the women around while they took care of it.

Happy to have companionship, Jack showed the women the new barn and the orchard, leading them toward the house. They were halted halfway by Jess calling to them, "Ya better come tell us where ya wanna put dis stuff. We ain't in no mood t' be movin' it 'round t' suit ya!"

"Cap'n, I reckon we gonna hafta put off seein' yer fine house," Cally said with spirit, heading in Jess's direction. "These men can't do nothin' wit'out us."

Jack forced a laugh, and with a wave of his hand he walked on. The setting sun was casting long shadows on the ground. When he entered the dim interior of the house, it matched his mood. Out of sight of the others, he sank into a chair, succumbing to the despair he had battled so long.

Why had he expected news of Cordelia? After all, he had not asked Jess to seek her out. But still he had hoped. Her presence seemed to appear before him as it had done so many times of late.

"Jack," her voice spoke softly to him.

He moaned and buried his face in his hands. "Oh, dear God—please don't let me lose my mind," he begged brokenly, trembling from head to toe.

"Jack," the voice said again, and he felt a light touch on his shoulder.

Jack lifted his head to see Cordelia standing before him, hands outstretched.

"I must be going mad!" he gasped.

"No, Jack—I'm real," she said softly. "Take my hand, and come with me." As one in a dream, Jack took her warm hand, allowing himself to be led to the front veranda.

"Cordelia, I can't believe it's really you!" he managed, unable to take his eyes off her. "I've imagined this so many times. Will you disappear?"

"No dearest—I'm here. I have no intention of leaving."

"When—how—?" Jack stammered.

"I came with Jess and Toby. I wanted to surprise you—I would have come sooner, but I didn't know—I'm sorry. When you left, no one knew where you had gone."

"When Stant told me you had gone back to Charleston, I thought you never wanted to see me again," Jack responded with an unsteady voice.

"At first I needed time, and I was worried about Hettie. Poor dear! Jack, they nearly killed her. It was days before she was found. She's getting better, but her mind's not the same. She's with Mary. I'll send money for her support. I've been trying desperately to find you—even wrote Colonel Stothard, but he hadn't heard from you and was worried also.

"I was nearly out of my mind with worry when Jess came to see me while he was in Charleston and told me where you were. He said—you had built a wonderful house for me and missed me something terrible.

"I came to see if that was true," she finished shyly, her violet eyes glowing in the twilight.

Jack felt his heart constrict as he gathered her tenderly in his arms. "My darling Cordelia, I have longed for you every day. All I have built would have meant nothing without you to share it with me. Will you marry me?"

Cordelia pushed herself back so she could see his face. "Andrew Jackson Brevard, I would be proud to be your wife," she whispered tremulously.

"Tomorrow?"

"Tomorrow would be wonderful—but perhaps we should wait for all your friends to be here."

"Whatever you wish," he murmured tenderly.

"In the meantime, we should take care of our chaperons," she gently reminded. "And speaking of chaperons, I expect they're getting as hungry as we are."

For the first time in months, Jack threw back his head and laughed.

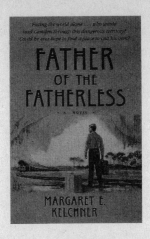

A SHADOW FROM THE HEAT

When Wes Scott leaves his home in Savannah, Georgia, in a desperate search for his wayward sister, Testa, who had run off with a "gamblin' man," little does he realize the long, perilous journey ahead. Deep into the vast reaches of the Southwest desert Testa's abuser flees, dragging her along—with Wes in relentless pursuit. Nearing starvation and without water, Wes comes face-to-face with the bitter reality that he might not survive the cruel elements and many other dangers of the frontier himself—much less save Testa.

Wes must cling to God's promise that He will be "a shadow from the heat." Will that promise be enough?

Can he save his sister and the woman he loves?
Can he save himself?

AT083-411-5158

Purchase from your local bookstore
Or order from
Beacon Hill Press of Kansas City
800-877-0700

NIGHTSONG

The setting is Castine, a small port village on Penobscot Bay in what is now the state of Maine. As the storm clouds portending the Revolutionary War grow in ferocity, the dangers that the citizens of Castine live with daily intensify—skirmishes with the fierce Abnaki Indians, piracy in the waters off their bay, and the harshness of the North Atlantic elements.

A trader along the Eastern seaboard, Capt. Matthew Jarden has carefully avoided trouble in his years of plying the sea—this despite strident opposition to the slave trade. But when a British-Indian alliance lays siege to Castine, just days after the death of his beloved wife, the proud captain becomes a hunted man with a bounty on his head. The only place more dangerous than Castine is his ship, and so reluctantly he smuggles his only daughter Rosa ashore, knowing too well the dangers that await her.

Nightsong is the story of Rosa Jarden's courageous fight to survive, to do what is right before God, to be part of the birth of a great nation.

Based on Revolutionary War events that occurred in and around Castine, Maine

AT083-411-5298

Purchase from your local bookstore
Or order from
Beacon Hill Press of Kansas City
800-877-0700